TRACKER

#1

THE WINNING HAND

Books by Robert J. Randisi

Tracker

TRACKER

#1

THE WINNING HAND

Robert J. Randisi

SPEAKING VOLUMES, LLC

NAPLES, FLORIDA

2011

TRACKER

#1 THE WINNING HAND

ISBN 978-1-61232-804-1

To my mother and father,
who have memories of me
as a baby;

to my brother and my sister,
who have memories of me as a
brute;

to my wife, Anna, who has always
been my main lady;

and to my son, Christopher, who
has always given me a boot.

I love ya all!

Prologue:

Arizona, 1881

Tracker scanned the cards on the table, carefully computing the odds in his favor before saying, "I raise," and threw in the last of his stake. He'd traveled a long way to play in this particular poker game and it had to be all or nothing.

As he'd expected, the remaining players all dropped out, except for one. The well-dressed dude they called Rhodes was seated directly opposite Tracker. He reached inside his jacket pocket now and withdrew a folded piece of paper, apparently some kind of document.

"I believe this will more than cover the amount of your bet, Mr. Tracker," he announced confidently.

"It's just Tracker," Tracker told him.

"Yes, well, uh—," the man said, extending the piece of paper to Tracker.

Rhodes was sitting with four hearts on the table in front of him, and Tracker had already decided that the man had the fifth one in the hole. He accepted the document and scanned it just long enough to identify it as what it was, then handed it to the man standing to his right.

"Duke, you've been to San Francisco," he told him. "Is this enough to cover my bet?"

Duke, who had never been more than a spectator at any poker game, and usually attended Tracker's, read the paper through and then handed it back to his friend, saying, "That should cover it."

Taking Duke's word, Tracker threw the paper into the pot and told Rhodes, "Okay, you've covered me."

The man seemed to be in a great rush to turn over his cards, and as he fumbled them over everyone in the room could see why. They were *all* hearts, all seven of them. He'd had his flush all along.

"How many times have you ever seen that?" the dude asked excitedly. "All hearts, not just five, but all of them! Ain't that a pretty sight? I just knew it was a sign," he told everyone, rubbing his hands together.

"Well, it may have been a sign of some kind," Tracker told him calmly, "but it sure as hell wasn't a sign of victory."

Tracker turned over only two of his three hole cards, but since they were both threes, and he had two more of them on the table, it was enough.

"Damn!" Rhodes snapped, slamming his hands down on the table, scattering his pretty array of hearts.

Tracker reached for the pot and raked it in. He picked up that piece of paper, folded it four times and stuffed it in his shirt pocket. After that he proceeded to sort his winnings.

The game was over.

"Congratulations, Mist—uh, Tracker," Rhodes told him. "You are the proud new owner of one of the finest little hotels in San Francisco."

All the players were on their feet now, scraping back their chairs, putting on jackets or strapping on guns, preparing to leave.

"Don't worry," Tracker told him, "I'll hold onto it long enough for you to redeem it."

"Redeem it?" Rhodes asked, walking around to Tracker's side of the table. "My dear Tracker, I have no intentions whatsoever of redeeming it. Quite the contrary, I've been trying to unload it for some time."

Tracker stopped in the act of strapping on his gunbelt when he heard the word "unload."

"Whoa, hold it a minute," he said. "What do you mean 'unload'? What's wrong with the place?"

Tracker turned to face his friend, Duke Farrell, and reminded him, "Duke, you told me the place was worth the bet."

Duke held up his hands and pushed them out towards Tracker and said, "Tracker, it's worth it, believe me."

Tracker, who at six-four was almost a full foot taller than his friend, peered down at the smaller man and said, "Oh, yeah? When was the last time you were in San Francisco?"

Duke thought a moment, then admitted grudgingly, "Well, it has been almost six months, but—"

"Shit!" Tracker snapped, the feeling that he'd been stiffed becoming stronger and stronger, "A hell of a lot could have happened in six months! The place could have burned down!"

Rhodes, who was himself a half a foot shorter than Tracker, put his hand on the big man's shoulder and attempted to allay his fears.

"Tracker, believe me, the hotel is still standing and is not even in a state of disrepair. When you get to San Francisco, you'll see that it really is well worth the amount of the bet."

"Oh, really?" Tracker asked. "Then why have you been looking to unload it? Why did you bet it, huh?"

Rhodes rubbed his hands over the stubble that had coated his face during the twenty-hour poker game.

"Well now, I've been looking to unload it simply because I am not cut out to be in the hotel business. As for why I bet it—," he went on, shrugging helplessly, "—hey, I'm a gambler, and I had seven hearts!" He held up seven fingers to illustrate his point and added, "What would you have done?"

Tracker hesitated a moment, then said, "I would have bet the hotel."

"Exactly. Tracker, I hope we have the opportunity to sit down at the same table again, some time," Rhodes told him.

Still not completely convinced he hadn't been taken, Tracker replied, "Sure, only next time do me a favor?"

"What's that?"

"Bring enough cash?"

"Uh, yes, of course. Gentlemen, good night," Rhodes said and left.

"Somebody ought to tell him it's morning," Duke Farrell commented.

"He'll find out when he gets outside," Tracker answered.

Both men walked over to Tom McClure, who had set the game up, and shook hands, bidding him good-bye.

"Nice game, Tom," Tracker told him.

"You *should* thank me," McClure told him. "You did all right for yourself, this time. Got yourself a nice new shiny hotel."

McClure was a tall skinny man with a protruding Adam's apple and a long, carefully cared for handlebar mustache.

"Yeah, well," Tracker said, touching the piece of paper in his shirt pocket, "I don't know how new it is, but at least I know it's a hotel." He looked pointedly at Duke Farrell and said, "Don't I?"

Duke and Tracker had a funny kind of friendship. They showed up in the same places at the same time an awful lot, and yet it was always—or mostly—by coincidence. They both gambled, but Duke never touched cards. He gambled on his ability to fool people, hoping to trick them out of enough money to keep him going until his next game. Tracker played cards, but Duke Farrell played people.

They were friends, that was true, but Tracker wasn't all that sure that Farrell was above playing him once or twice.

And this might be one of those times.

"Tracker," Duke told him now, "it's good, believe me. I wouldn't tell you it was if it wasn't."

The expression of his face was so "honest" that Tracker couldn't help but be suspicious.

"Duke—," he began, but McClure cut him off.

"Can I see that?" he asked.

"Sure, Tom," Tracker said, and handed the paper over.

"'Rhodes House,'" McClure read out loud. "I think I know this place, Tracker. If it's the one I think, you may have done better for yourself than you think," he said, handing the paper back.

"You think so?"

"I do. It ain't one of the biggest hotels in San Francisco, but it's still a damned fine place." Rubbing his jaw, McClure said, "In fact, if you really find that you don't want this place, I might be willing to take it off your hands. I think I can give you a fair price."

"Is that so?" Tracker read the paper over himself, then asked, "Rhodes, that was the dude's name, right?"

"Right, Carl Rhodes. He's a gambler all the way. Makes his living from it. In fact, I wouldn't be surprised if he got that hotel the same way he lost it," McClure said.

Tracker seemed to consider his options for a moment, then returned the paper to his pocket.

"Thanks for the offer, Tom. I'll think about it and let you know."

"Sure, Tracker. Let me know what you decide. See you boys later." He nodded to both of them and left.

"You see?" Duke demanded when McClure was gone. "You're always so damned suspicious of your friends."

"Not all my friends, Duke," Tracker replied, "only you."

"Amounts to the same thing," Duke reminded him, and Tracker had to admit that the little man was right. He'd be hard put to name another friend after Duke Farrell.

"So, what are you gonna do with your hotel, Tracker?" Duke asked him.

Tracker shrugged.

"I think the first thing I should do is go to San Francisco and take a look at it and see just what it is I own."

Just as he said that, however, he was struck by an idea.

"Duke," he said, laying a powerful arm on his friend's thin shoulders, "how would you like me to buy you dinner?"

"What's the catch?" Duke asked immediately.

"Now who's being suspicious of his friends?" Tracker asked. "There's no catch," he assured the ace con man. "I just might want you to do me a little favor, that's all."

"That's all, huh? What kind of favor, and what's it going to cost me?"

Tracker beamed at his friend from a face that was not built for beaming and said, "How would you like to own a hotel?"

"But you just told Tom you didn't want to sell the hotel—"

Tracker patted Duke on the back and told him, "Come along with me and I'll explain at dinner."

Chapter 1

At the ripe old age of thirty-four, the man known as Tracker had a lot of miles on him, which might make some people find it odd that he had never before been to San Francisco. At six-four and two-forty he had never been intimidated by the sheer size of anyone or anything before, and this was a totally new experience for him. He was slightly awed by the size of the city itself, and by the amount of activity that was going on around him as he rode in.

He reined in the dapple gray he had named Two-Pair after the hand he had been holding when he won him three years ago. He had been offered a lot of money for the animal over the years, but had never been tempted to sell him.

Tracker stopped a man in the street and asked him for directions to the livery stable.

"Which one?" the man asked.

"How many are there?" Tracker asked, surprised.

When the man took too long, obviously trying to figure in his head just how many there were, Tracker said, "Never mind, friend. Why don't you just point me to the nearest one?"

The man's face brightened and he gladly gave the directions Tracker had requested.

"Would that be anywhere near a hotel called Rhodes House?" he asked then.

"Rhodes House?" the man repeated, rubbing his lean jaw. "Oh, you mean Farrell House? Why, shore, it's jest about four or five blocks from there."

Most towns Tracker had ever been in weren't even four or five blocks long all told.

"Farrell House?" Tracker asked, to be sure he'd heard the man correctly.

"Yep. They got a new owner over there and he upped and changed the name first thing. Right nice place, too."

"Much obliged for the information," Tracker told him and wheeled Two-Pair around to head for the livery.

Tracker dropped some extra cash on the boy attendant to make sure the gray would be well cared for and fed, and then collected his gear and headed for "Farrell House" to check in.

His first impression upon seeing the place was that there must have been some mistake. Although it was by no means the largest building he'd seen during his very short time in San Francisco, it was larger than any *hotel* he'd ever seen, or stayed in.

Walking inside he was further impressed by the size of the front lobby, and then he suddenly became angry with himself for acting like it was his first day off the farm. He'd been to large towns before, this one was just a mite larger than usual. In fact, when he considered his own size, this town might just fit him better than most.

Tracker approached the front desk and dropped his bedroll to the floor. The little dandy behind the desk looked at him over his wire-rimmed glasses and decided that he couldn't possibly be wanting a room here.

"Can I help you?" he asked the big man, and then added, "sir?" as an afterthought.

The clerk was confident in his own mind that he certainly would not be able to help this ... this ... ruffian.

"Yes," Tracker said, shattering that bubble, "I have a reservation."

14

"A reservation?"

"That's right," Tracker repeated, "a reservation."

"Oh, I see," the clerk said doubtfully. "Well, uh, could I have your name, please?"

"Tracker."

"Uh, your first name?"

"No, it's my last name."

"No, I mean, what is your first name?"

"Just look under Tracker," the big man told him.

The clerk was about forty or thereabouts, and couldn't have been much taller than five-three. Among other things, Tracker expected that his neck was beginning to hurt him from looking up the way he was. The little man checked his reservation list and—as he had suddenly feared—found Tracker's name.

"Uh, yes, Mister Tracker—"

"Just Tracker."

The clerk looked like his whole world was coming apart as he said, "Ah, yes, as you wish—"

"Is there something wrong with my reservation?" Tracker asked, leaning on the counter.

"Oh, uh, no, sir," the clerk said, backing away involuntarily, "nothing at all. Front!" he shouted, his voice a high squeak.

Tracker wondered who the guy was calling and then found a kid in some kind of a uniform at his elbow.

"Uh, this fellow will carry your, uh, bag and show you to your room, sir," the clerk told him.

"Don't I look big enough to carry my own gear?" Tracker asked him.

"No, sir, uh, I mean, yes, sir, but—"

"In fact," Tracker pointed out, gesturing to each of them in turn, "I could probably carry him, my gear and you."

The little clerk seemed to take the remark as a threat and backed away from the bigger man as much as he could.

"I meant no offense, sir," he told Tracker hastily.

"None taken," Tracker told him. He picked up his bedroll and rifle and told the kid, "Lead on, friend."

His room was huge but he'd steeled himself against that eventuality so that he would not be overly impressed.

15

He threw the kid a coin and the kid said, "Thanks, Mister. You need anything while you're here—booze, girls—anything at all, you let me know, huh?"

The kid looked barely sixteen, but his eyes looked years older and Tracker was sure that he'd be able to deliver just about anything he promised.

"You supply everything?" Tracker asked him.

"Just about," the kid said, proudly.

"Do me a favor, then," Tracker told him, tossing him another coin that the kid deftly caught. "Find the owner of this hotel and tell him that Tracker has checked in."

"The owner?" the kid asked. "You mean Mr. Farrell, or—"

"Yeah, Farrell," Tracker interrupted.

"Just tell him you're checked in?"

"That's right."

"You know Mr. Farrell?" the kid asked.

"Just deliver the message, kid, and then get me a bottle of whiskey, okay?"

Tracker tossed him still another coin, and the kid said, "You got it, Mister."

"The name's Tracker, kid."

When the kid left, Tracker sat on the bed and tried to convince himself that he really owned this hotel. He'd never owned anything he couldn't carry himself, or strap to the back of a horse and take with him.

"What the hell am I going to do with a hotel this size?" he asked himself aloud.

Chapter 2

Tracker got his bottle about twenty minutes later, but it wasn't the kid who brought it.

When the knock came on his door he asked who it was.

"Room service," a feminine voice called out.

Frowning, he opened the door and found a girl standing there with a bottle of whiskey.

"You asked for this, didn't you?" she asked, holding the bottle up while Tracker looked over her. She was tall, and the heels she was wearing made her even taller. Tracker liked tall women, and he liked his women the way this one was built: tall, lean, good breasts, long legs, and an interesting face. Not exactly beautiful, but very interesting. Full lips, a nose that would have been too big on another woman, but was just right for her face, high cheekbones and long, black-as-night hair.

Tracker was suspicious of the fact that she was built as if he had personally ordered her. Duke knew his taste in women, and Tracker assumed that she had been sent by his friend, the little con man.

17

"Are you supposed to distract me for a while?" he asked, taking the bottle from her.

"I'm supposed to help you fill your time," she told him, pouting. "Aren't you going to let me in, or do you want me to get fired?"

He hesitated a moment, looking her over again, then said, "Come in, then. I don't want to be responsible for getting you fired."

She walked in and shut the door behind her.

"Drink?" he asked her.

"Just a short one."

He looked around, then turned to her and shrugged. "No glasses."

"That's okay," she assured him. She walked up to him, took the bottle, opened it and very deliberately put her full lips over the top and took a short pull. When she finished she handed it back to him, licking her lips very slowly, making them glisten invitingly.

The look on her face was challenging, and Tracker had never been a man to turn down a challenge, especially from a woman.

"What's your name?" he asked her.

"Nora."

"Well, Nora, why don't we just forget the games, huh?" he suggested.

He grabbed her by the shoulders and pulled her to him, kissing her on the mouth. Her breath caught in surprise, but she adjusted quickly enough and thrust her tongue into his mouth. He slid the straps of her dress off her shoulders and worked her breasts free. They were not overly large, but they were firm and round, with brown nipples which he tweaked to life with his fingers.

When she began to writhe against him, grinding her pelvis against his, he pushed her away and said, "Get undressed."

She eyed him defiantly for a moment, then decided it wasn't worth arguing. For some reason, she wanted to be in this man's bed. She took off the remainder of her clothes. By the time she was naked so was he. He grabbed her to him again, kissing her hard, running his hands down her bare back until he was kneading the flesh of her firm buttocks. The power she felt in his

18

hand excited her and she wished he would take her to his bed already.

As if he had read her mind he turned her around and lowered her to the bed. He laid down alongside her and just as she was preparing herself for some rough sex, he went gentle on her, and that excited her even more. He ran his tongue over her breasts and nipples, teasing her with gentleness, while his right hand played between her legs, lighting a fire inside her.

"Oh, God," she moaned, "I want it, I want it..."

But Tracker wasn't ready to give it to her, not yet. She had been too cool, too confident when she came to his door, and he was going to make her beg for her fulfillment.

He continued to work her with his hand, while his lips roamed about her face, her neck, her breasts, and gradually he began to work his way down until his lips and tongue replaced his fingers.

When she felt his lips close around her she thrust her pelvis up into him, crying out in short gasps, "Oh, oh..."

He reached under her and grasped her buttocks, kneading them as he worked her with his mouth.

"Oh, God," she said, "please, put it in me, please, God..."

"Ask again," he told her. "Beg for it."

"Please, please...," she told him over and over until he moved atop her and plunged himself deep inside her.

Her breath caught and for a moment he thought she would never breathe again, but as he long-stroked her, her breath began to come in short gasps. As he increased his tempo so the tempo of her breathing increased, until finally she came, lifting both of them off the bed as she arched her back.

Still hard, even after she had relaxed, he continued stroking her in and out, long strokes, and then short, quick ones until he worked her up to her peak again, and this time they came together...

Afterwards he asked her, "Did Farrell send you up here?"

"Yes."

"What do you think of your new owner, Mr. Farrell?"

She shrugged.

"He's okay, I guess. I've seen worse. I know Lewis hates him, though," she told him.

"Who's Lewis?"

She made a face and said, "That little dandy on the desk. He says Mr. Farrell is 'vulgar', whatever that means."

"Somehow, I don't think Lewis had all that high an opinion of me, either," he told her. "You don't work in the hotel, do you?"

"Not exactly. The saloon where I work is part of the hotel. You get there through the dining room, or from outside."

"Well, then, why don't you go back to work, Nora? I'm expecting your boss up here soon."

"All right," she replied, meekly. She rose and he watched her dress, knowing that he had completely won her over. Once she was dressed she said, "If you need me again..."

"I know where to find you," he assured her.

She nodded, as if in a daze. It wasn't until she left the room and was standing out in the hallway that her mind really cleared.

She realized that the big man inside was a very special person. No one had ever quite used her the way he had before, and made her enjoy it so thoroughly.

He was a very special kind of man, indeed.

Chapter 3

When the next knock on the door came, Tracker knew it was Duke.

"Well, look at you," he said as he opened the door, stepping back to take a good look.

Duke was spruced from head to toe, with a new haircut, trimmed neater and shorter than Tracker had ever seen it before. He was also wearing the prettiest new suit you'd ever want to see. He looked every inch the high-class gambler.

And there was something else.

"Whoee!" Tracker said, sniffing the air. "What's that smell? What the hell are you wearing?"

"Hey, listen," the little man said, offended. "When you own a big hotel like this, you gotta look the part, right?"

"Oh, really?" Tracker asked. "When *you* own a big hotel?"

Looking sheepish, Duke said, "Well, you know, as far as anyone in town knows, I own it—that's all I meant."

"You sure picked out a pretty name for it, didn't you?" Tracker asked.

Duke's mouth opened and closed a couple of times as he tried to think of a good explanation.

"Okay, okay, come inside and close the door before someone sees you."

Duke entered the room and closed the door behind him.

"How did you like your present?" he asked Tracker.

"You mean Nora?"

"Yeah, ain't she something?"

"She was fine, Duke, just fine."

"How do you like this place?" Duke asked, waving his arms to indicate the room. "It's the biggest room in the place."

"Thanks a heap," Tracker told him, "but I didn't want to attract any attention, remember?"

Tracker opened his whiskey bottle and took a healthy pull.

"If you came into the hotel dressed like that," Duke told him, "and as big as you are, you know you attracted plenty of attention."

"Especially from that dandy you've got on the desk," Tracker told him.

"Lewis? He came with the hotel, Tracker. I haven't really made any personnel changes. I didn't want to do that without asking you first."

"Too bad you didn't feel that way about changing the name."

"Ah, I knew you wouldn't want it to go on being called Rhodes House, would you?"

"No, you got that right."

"And you wouldn't have liked it if I had called the place Tracker's, would you?"

"Okay, Duke, we'll drop it for now." Tracker surrendered.

Frowning, Duke said, "Hey, what's the matter with you? You look like you don't like your place. This is great!"

Tracker sat on the bed with the bottle and, after another big pull on it, said, "It's fine, Duke, just fine, but it's a hell of a lot more than I expected. You never told me enough to prepare me for this."

Duke smiled broadly and said, "I wish I could have seen your face when you first laid eyes on the place. Surprised, huh?"

"Oh, I was surprised all right," Tracker told him, standing up, "and I didn't like the feeling."

Duke backed away from his friend, who looked fairly menacing at that moment. Not that he was afraid of Tracker, but it didn't hurt to be careful.

"Now don't get mad, Tracker," Duke cautioned his friend, holding his hands up in front of him, palms out.

"I'm not mad, Duke. Settle down."

Duke dropped his hands and took a relaxing breath.

"This is just going to take some getting used to, that's all," Tracker continued. "Why don't you tell me what you've found, so far?"

Duke was a good con man which, in most cases, translated into being a good business man. He'd once acted as a bank manager for two weeks and actually had the bank showing more of a profit before he finally took off with a large bundle of cash. Tracker had figured on sending Duke in ahead of him to see what kind of shape the hotel was in. He really had no overriding desire to be a hotel owner and wanted to stay in the background as long as possible.

He was paying Duke to act out his part, but the little man was doing it as more of a favor.

"I can give you a complete rundown later tonight, Tracker. Why don't you get a bath and something to eat downstairs? I'll have one of the boys bring you up some hot water."

"Bring it up?"

"Sure. You've got a tub right in there," Duke told him, pointing to a closed door.

"All the rooms have tubs?" Tracker asked.

"Not all of them, just some of the larger ones."

"You mean the more expensive ones, don't you?"

He nodded. "That, too."

"Okay," Tracker agreed. "I'll get cleaned up and have some supper, then I want you up here to fill me in, and Duke—"

"What?"

"—you better give it to me straight."

"Hey, Tracker, come on!" Duke scolded his friend.

"Look, after your bath get dressed in some of the clothes I bought for you."

"You bought me clothes?"

"Yeah, they're in there," Duke said, pointing to a closet. "San Francisco style, you know? You got to look the part."

"Do I have to smell like you, too?" Tracker asked scornfully.

Duke gave his big friend a reproachful look, then started for the door, saying, "I'll leave word in the dining room that you're not to be charged. Best steaks in San Francisco."

When Duke left, Tracker took an extra long pull on the whiskey bottle, and then replaced the cap.

Baths, dining rooms, new clothes, he thought. He walked to the closet, opened it and fingered some of the clothes. He took out one of the suits and laid it out on the bed, trying to picture himself in it.

I'm never going to be able to get used to this, he told himself.

Chapter 4

Finally, it was remembering the desk clerk's reaction to him that made Tracker decide to go ahead and wear one of the suits. He picked out the plainest one of the bunch and put it on. It was a perfect fit, which was no surprise because Duke knew his size.

He examined the tall, blond-haired gent in the mirror and decided that he didn't look half bad. He strapped on his Colt and it kind of spoiled the picture, but he wasn't about to go around without it. He was on too many people's lists to do that.

On the top shelf of the closet he found a black, straight-brimmed hat with a silver band. It wasn't exactly his style, but it went with the suit, so he put it on. The suit jacket covered his worn holster. The only thing that showed was the butt of his .45. Satisfied with his appearance, he went down to get some dinner.

He was shown to a table by a waiter who told him that he couldn't have a drink because they did not serve "alcoholic beverages" in the dining room. He suggested that while Tracker's dinner was cooking he "repair" to the saloon for his before-dinner drink.

Tracker decided to do that, as much to take a look around as for a drink.

The dining room was full of well-dressed people having polite conversation. The men all wore suits, and the women all wore gowns and makeup, although for most of them it didn't help their appearances any. It had always seemed to him that the worse a woman looked, the more paint they covered themselves with. They should take after Indian women, he thought, who wore no makeup, and didn't need any.

Even dressed as he was, he felt out of place. A couple of times he caught some of them looking his way. Could they tell he didn't belong in the clothes he was wearing? Or were they discussing the wisdom of wearing a big Colt Walker with a three-piece suit?

Tracker passed through a doorway at the far end of the room and passed into what was for him the normal world. The saloon looked just about like any other. A little larger, perhaps, and a little better kept, but it was still a saloon.

He didn't see Nora around, although there were some girls circulating. He went up to the bar and ordered a beer.

"Sure thing, Mister," the bartender told him. The man was huge, a couple of inches taller than Tracker, and about thirty pounds heavier. He had massive, heavily muscled arms, and thick, sloping shoulders. He set the beer down in front of Tracker and said, "New in town?"

"Just got in today," Tracker told him. He took a couple of swallows of the good, cold brew and then said, "Hey, listen."

"Yeah?"

"I ordered a steak in the dining room next door and, uh, I was wondering—"

"You'd rather eat it in here?" the man asked.

"Yeah, how'd you know?"

"Ah, I knew you wasn't the type who could sit in there and eat comfortable. Too ritzy, too many fancy dans and their women. You look like a two-fisted eater,

Mister, and I don't think you'd be able to pack it in the way you like if you was sitting in there."

"You're right about that," Tracker told him.

"Take a table, friend. I'll have your dinner brought in here. No problem," the bartender assured him.

"Much obliged."

Tracker watched as the man walked from behind the bar to arrange it. He had hands like hams and legs like tree trunks. His hair was black, peppered liberally with gray, and he looked like he was an ex-fighter just gone past forty, or more.

By the time Tracker had sat himself at a table the man was coming back carrying a heaping plate.

"I told the cook—oh, pardon me, the 'chef'—to pile on some extra spuds and vegetables."

"Thanks."

"Eat hearty, friend."

Tracker proceeded to do just that.

"Mind if I set?" the man asked then.

Tracker looked up at him, then said, "Be my guest."

"My name's Will Sullivan, friend," he said, introducing himself.

"Tracker," he answered around a mouthful of meat and potatoes.

"Tracker, you ever do any fighting?" Sullivan asked.

Tracker washed his food down with a mouthful of beer and said, "Well, I've never been known to back away from one."

"I mean professional, like in the ring. Boxing," the man clarified.

"I've sparred some, yeah," Tracker told him. Fact of the matter was, Tracker was a damned good fighter, and even enjoyed a good fight. What he didn't approve of was getting paid to beat some poor soul's brains in, and having a hundred people yelling and screaming for him to do it.

"Good. I got a proposition for you."

"What kind of proposition?"

"Well, as you could probably tell, I'm a fighter," Sullivan told him, showing him his well-scarred knuckles.

"I was thinking that maybe you *was* a fighter," Tracker told him honestly.

"Oh, yeah," Sullivan said, touching his hair, "the

gray." He waved it away. "Makes me look older than I am."

"How old are you?"

"I'm...thirty-eight."

Tracker looked at him, the doubt painted clearly on his face, and Sullivan said, "All right, I'm forty...three, but I've still got it where it counts," he assured Tracker, closing his massive hands into fists. "I've got a match set up for the end of next week that's going to put me right back in the heavyweight picture." He moved his chair closer to the table and lowered his voice, adding, "That's where you come in."

"Where?" Tracker asked, pushing away his empty plate and grabbing up his beer.

"Another beer?" Sullivan asked. "On the house?"

"How could I refuse?" Tracker asked. He drained his mug and handed it to Sullivan. The big man—one of the few men Tracker had ever seen who was bigger than himself—went and got another mugful, then returned and told Tracker, "I need a sparring mate."

"Look, Sullivan—" Tracker began.

"Will, call me Will."

"Okay, Will, I said I've sparred some—"

"Tracker, look, you're a big man, near as big as me. Your hands are almost as big as mine. There ain't no one else in this town that fits that description. I need you, Tracker. I'll pay you—"

"How much?" Tracker asked, just out of curiosity.

"Well, after I win my purse—"

"Wait a minute," Tracker said. "You want me to get into the ring with you so you can practice by beating my brains out, and I don't get paid unless you win?"

"Oh, don't worry about that," Will Sullivan told him, "I'm going to win, all right."

"You are, huh?"

"Oh, come on, Tracker. Don't tell me you don't need the money, and don't tell me you ain't a gambling man. I mean, I know you're wearing a fancy suit and all, but that worn holster and forty-five are more your style."

He was right about that, Tracker had to admit—half of it, anyway. The gun and holster were more his style, but about needing the money—Tracker wondered what Sullivan would say if he told the boxer that he

28

owned the hotel and the saloon and that as a bartender he—Sullivan—worked for Tracker.

But he wasn't going to tell him that.

In fact, he was going to take him up on his offer, just for the hell of it.

"Where's your camp?" Tracker asked.

"Uh, yeah, my camp," the boxer said, scratching his head, looking sheepish. "Well, I haven't got a place yet—"

"You've got a fight the end of next week and you haven't started training yet?"

"Oh, no, I didn't mean that," Sullivan assured him. "I'm in shape. I'm as strong as an ox. I been running and all, I just haven't been able to get myself a, uh, worthy sparring partner."

Tracker frowned at the man's choice of words and had the feeling the problem had not been not getting "worthy" partners, but getting any at all. He decided to let the question go until another time.

"Well, you've got one now," he told the boxer.

"Hey, no kidding?" the man asked happily. "You didn't even ask how much I'd pay you."

"Yeah, I did. You avoided the question," he reminded him.

"Oh, yeah, that's right."

"How about we celebrate with another beer?" he asked.

"On the house," Sullivan told him.

"I wouldn't have it any other way," Tracker assured him.

Sullivan brought the beer back and said, "Now all we gotta do is find someplace to set up a ring."

"You know, Will," Tracker told him, raising his glass, "somehow I don't think that's going to be a problem."

Chapter 5

"You want to do *what?*" Duke asked incredulously.

"I want to set up a boxing ring somewhere in the hotel," he told his friend again. "We've got room someplace, don't we?"

"Well, I suppose, but—"

"How about the dining room? That big enough?" Tracker suggested.

"The dining room? Do you know how much money that dining room brings in a day?" Duke asked, looking stricken at the idea of closing it down.

"No, I don't," Tracker told him. "That's what you're supposed to be telling me right now."

"Yeah, well, this can wait," Duke said, closing the ledger he was about to show Tracker. "I got something else to tell you."

"What?" Tracker asked, immediately suspicious.

"It's about your ownership of the hotel," Duke told him.

"What about it? I own it, don't I?"

"Well, yes...and no."

"What does that mean, Duke?" Tracker demanded. "Come on, spit it out. Don't tell me that dude Rhodes took me."

"No, no, he didn't take you, Tracker...but he didn't tell you everything either."

"You're beating around the goddamned bush, Duke!" Tracker bellowed.

"Okay, okay, but don't get sore!"

"I'm not getting sore!"

"Like hell you're not!"

Tracker started to snap back but caught himself. He took a deep breath and said, "Okay, now I'm not sore. Give it to me straight, Duke."

"You own the place, Tracker, but there's also another owner."

"Who?"

"A girl."

"A girl owns my hotel?"

"Well, I guess you could say you own her hotel."

"Duke—"

"Let me explain the situation."

"That's what I've been waiting for."

"Basically, you and the girl own the hotel half-and-half. Seems her father started the place and when Rhodes came along and won it—like we figured—he signed a piece of paper saying that the old man's daughter would always own half-interest. Kind of a sentimental thing, you know?"

"Sentimental? You mean, it's not legal?" Tracker asked.

"Oh, I think it's legal, all right."

"Okay, hold it," Tracker said, holding up one hand. "Give me a chance to take this all in."

He still owned the hotel, but not all of it. He had a partner, a girl. That was it? That didn't seem so bad.

"What's her name?"

"Deirdre Long," Duke told him. "She's a pretty little filly, Tracker, but as feisty as they come. Stubborn, you know? Doesn't want anything changed. Bitched like hell when I changed the name of the place."

"Maybe she was bitching about what you changed it to," Tracker suggested. "You say she's got a piece of paper?"

31

"Yeah."

Tracker shook his head.

"Too many damned pieces of paper floating around," he told his friend. There was the one Rhodes had given Tracker, the one Rhodes had given the girl, and the one Tracker had given Duke that said *he* was the owner. There was also a piece of paper strictly between Duke and Tracker saying that Duke was Tracker's representative in hotel matters.

"Somewhere along the line I'd like to see her piece of paper," Tracker told Duke.

"You ready to step forward as owner?" Duke asked.

Tracker thought about that.

"No, I'm not," he finally said, "and I may never be. Duke, if I decide to keep the place I may want you to stay on and run it for me."

"That's fine with me, I'm having a ball, but why?"

"This isn't for me," Tracker told him, opening his arms to indicate everything, "but I do kind of like the idea of owning it—or part of it, anyway. Is the split down the middle?"

"Just about. She's got forty-nine percent, and you've got fifty-one, which is why I was able to change the name of the hotel even though she was dead set against it."

"Okay, fine, then we can do what we want."

"Not without a fight," Duke warned him.

"I can handle a slip of a girl," Tracker assured him.

"That I got to see," Duke told him, smiling.

"Don't worry. Okay, so if we can't use the dining room as a boxing ring, what can I use?"

"That again? What the hell do you want that for?"

Tracker explained it to him and Duke shook his head.

"He's over the hill, Tracker. Poor guy's punch drunk, thinking he can come back. He's almost fifty. The guy he's supposed to fight is half his age, and a local favorite. What do you want to get involved for?"

"It appeals to me, Duke. I like the guy. What room can we use?" he asked again.

Duke let some air out through his mouth and said, "Well, it's your hotel. There's a storeroom behind the dining room. It's plenty big enough to put a ring in."

"Okay, great," Tracker said enthusiastically. "I'll tell Will and we can start putting it up tomorrow."

"Wait a minute," Duke said. "What am I gonna tell Deirdre? This boxing business ain't gonna sit too well with her, I'll tell you that right now."

Tracker stopped at the door of his room with his hand on the knob and said, "Tell her you bought yourself a piece of a fighter. She'll think you're a big investor."

"Sure, but what about the books?" his friend said, holding up the ledger. "Don't you want to see them?"

"How do they look to you?"

"Me? They look fine to me. They balance, if that's what you mean. The hotel shows a profit consistently."

"Fine, I'll take your word for it," Tracker told him and left.

He decided to take the side stairs down. That way he could enter the saloon without having to go through the dining room. When he came out into the dark alley something whacked him behind the ear and he went down, but not out. Reacting on pure instinct, he kicked out with his boot, catching someone on the shin. Whoever it was cried out in pain and staggered back. Tracker struggled to his feet in time to catch somebody else's fist in his stomach. The blow drove him back against the wall and told him that he was dealing with more than one attacker. All he could make out in the shadows were two darkened figures, and one of them came towards him as he slouched against the wall. He balled up his fists and drove the right one forward, hoping to catch the man in the face. His fist glanced off the top of his opponent's head, probably doing more damage to his hand than to the other's head. At least it drove the man back a few steps, giving Tracker a chance to straighten up.

"Get him, damnit!" somebody hissed, and it wasn't one of the two men who had attacked him. Apparently there was a noncombatant third party present who didn't like the way things were going.

Tracker stood straight up now and planted his feet firmly, balling both fists again. When the two men came in together he began trading blows with them, taking two for every one he landed.

"Shit, come and help us, Frank," one of the men hissed.

"Don't say my name, damnit!" the third man called back in anger, but he finally stepped forward to help, and Tracker was dealing with six fists now. They were starting to wear him down, so he decided to change his tactics. He spread his arms wide, took a few free shots in the face for his trouble and then charged forward with a loud bellow. He caught them off balance and took all three of them to the ground with him. He felt somebody's head up against him and proceeded to butt him as hard as he could. He'd always had a thick skull, and it worked to his advantage as a wide gash appeared on the other man's forehead.

"Oh, Jesus," the injured man cried out.

Tracker stopped punching and kicking and tried to roll away so that he could draw his gun. Even if he couldn't see them clearly he might get lucky and hit one of them, or scare them away.

He rolled a couple of times, but as he went for his gun something hit him in the back of the head again, same spot behind the ear, and his head started to swim. Before he could successfully clear it he felt someone's foot on the back of his neck, pressing his face into the ground.

"Grab him now!" the voice of the man called Frank yelled out. "Come on, I can't hold him forever."

The other two men reacted to his commands and they each grabbed one of Tracker's arms, pulling them straight up behind him. They also each planted a boot firmly against the small of his back, as if they'd performed the same maneuver before. Once they had him, the third man removed his boot from the back of Tracker's neck. Tracker continued to struggle until the man called Frank pressed the barrel of a gun against his temple.

"Lie still, friend, or I'll blow your brains out," he whispered in Tracker's ear.

Tracker obeyed and it suddenly became very quiet in the alley. He could hear the three of them breathing hard.

"I've got some advice for you, stranger, and you better listen good and take heed. Are you listening?" Frank

34

asked, prodding the helpless Tracker with his gun. Tracker tried to answer but he couldn't speak very well. The man seemed to get the message, however, because he said, "That's good. Okay, here it is." He leaned closer and Tracker could smell stale beer and cigarettes on his breath.

"Stay away from Will Sullivan. Forget about sparring with him, or helping him get ready for his match in any way. You got that? Stay away from that old pug, or he might end up a dead pug—and you with him!"

Tracker was about to attempt some kind of a reply when the gun was removed from his temple and brought down on the back of his head.

On that same spot.

This time, he went out...

Chapter 6

Consciousness was elusive for Tracker, but when it finally came—or rather, when he finally captured it—it was worth the effort.

Standing above him was a young blond girl, very pretty and well built, wearing a blue dress with a high collar. Standing next to her was Duke.

He craned his head and found that he was lying on the bed in his hotel suite.

"How do you feel?" the girl asked.

Tracker worked his jaw, flexed his hands, arms and legs and said, "I seem to be in one piece, thanks. Duke?" he said, asking for an explanation.

"One of the guests discovered you in the alley and called me," Duke explained. "I got some help and had you carried up here."

Tracker exchanged glances with his friend, then looked pointedly at the blond girl.

"Tracker, this is Deirdre Long," Duke said by way of introduction. "Miss Long, this is my friend, Tracker."

"I assumed he was your friend, Mr. Farrell," she said

coldly. "I notice that he is not being charged for this suite, or for the meal he had from the dining room. Would you care to explain that?" she asked.

Duke ignored her question and said to Tracker, "Miss Long is partial owner of the hotel, Tracker."

"I see."

"She saw us carrying you up here and became, uh, quite curious."

"To say the least," Deirdre Long put in. Tracker looked at her again. He decided that she was not as young as he had first thought, putting her age at about twenty-four, and he also decided that she had the most beautiful blue eyes he had ever seen.

He told her so, and she regarded him critically.

"You are either a smooth talker, Mr. Tracker," she finally said, "or you've taken a rather bad bump on the head. I will give you time to recover before I decide which." She turned and gave Duke Farrell a cold stare and said, "I would still like an explanation, when you get a chance, Mr. Farrell."

Duke drew himself up nicely and said, "I'll talk to you later, Deirdre."

"Miss Long," she retorted, and then walked to the door and left the room without further word.

"Fiery, ain't she?" Tracker asked, propping himself up on his elbows.

"I told you so," Duke reminded him.

"Yeah," Tracker said, pushing himself up to a sitting position, "so you did. Ooh," he said as his bruises protested.

"You want to tell me what happened down there in the alley?" Duke asked.

"Three men jumped me, two at first, and I was doing pretty well until the third stepped in and hit me from behind."

"Did you see them?"

"No, it was too dark, but I heard a name."

"What name?"

"Frank."

"That's it?"

Tracker nodded and said, "Just Frank. After they had me down, this guy Frank warned me to stay away from Will Sullivan."

"Shit," Duke said in disgust. "I was hoping you'd forget about Sullivan, but now I know you won't. This man Frank picked the wrong man to try and warn off with a beating."

"You've got that right," Tracker replied. He stood up and stretched, trying to work out the bruises and kinks in his big body.

"I'm sure I split one of their foreheads open," he said to Duke. "We've got to find a guy named Frank, or a man with a crease on his forehead."

"Whoever the guy is you split open, he's bound to stay out of sight for a while."

"Maybe, and maybe not. We'll soon see. Where's my gun?" he asked.

"On the chair," Duke said, pointing.

Tracker went over, took his gunbelt and buckled it on. He looked around for his fancy hat, found it, brushed it off and put it on, then did the same with his coat.

"Where are you going?"

"Same place I was going before I got waylaid, but this time I've got some more questions for Will Sullivan."

Before leaving he picked up the bottle of whiskey he'd ordered earlier and took a couple of swallows.

Chapter 7

Tracker went through the hotel lobby this time, through the dining room and into the saloon. He saw Deirdre Long seated in the dining room, eating dinner, but did not stop to speak to her. She saw him, but did not even nod her head in recognition. He silently wished Duke luck telling her something she would accept, at least for a while.

When he entered the saloon he was gratified to find Sullivan still behind the bar.

"Hey, Tracker," the boxer called. When Tracker approached the bar Sullivan said in a lower voice, "Beer on the house? You look like you could use it."

Tracker examined himself in the mirror behind the bar, and agreed that he looked a mess. He had a bruise on his cheek, and there was a scrape above one eye. He removed his hat, placed it on the bar and ran one long-fingered hand through his mop of blond hair.

When Sullivan set the beer in front of him he took it and drained half of it gratefully.

"What happened?" Sullivan asked.

Tracker explained to Sullivan what had happened in the alley, and told him what "Frank" had said.

"Do you have any idea who this man Frank might be?" he finished.

Sullivan, looking puzzled and frowning mightily, shook his head and answered, "I ain't got the slightest notion, Tracker."

"Well, who'd want to hurt your chances in this fight?"

Sullivan smiled and said, "Guess somebody must think I got a chance of winning, huh?" He seemed delighted with the idea that someone other than himself thought he had a chance. "Maybe it's somebody who intends to bet on the other boy," he offered.

Tracker took another sip of beer and asked, "Who is this other boy?"

Sullivan shrugged and said, "Some local kid," but Tracker knew there was more to it than that.

"What aren't you telling me, Will?" he asked.

"What are you, some kind of a mind reader?" Sullivan asked. He was frowning, but then he smiled and seemed to realize that he would have to tell his new friend the truth if he expected to get any help.

"The kid's name is Homer Barrow, only they call him 'Battling Barrow.'"

"How old is he?"

"Ah, twenty-two or three. Just a kid. I got all the experience. He won't give me any trouble."

"Well, somebody seems to want to give you trouble before you even get in the ring," Tracker said. "What's his background?"

"What do you mean?"

"Has he got any family? Come on, Will, quit stalling and tell me the whole story."

"Okay, okay, Tracker," Sullivan told him. He leaned his massive forearms on the bar and started to explain.

"The kid's old man is a big wheel in this town. He owns a big gambling hall and saloon, among other things."

"Like what?"

"Like people," Sullivan said, making a face. "He's got so much money he thinks he can buy anybody."

"Did he try and buy you?" Tracker asked.

Sullivan smiled and said, "You're pretty smart,

Tracker. Yeah, he tried to pay me off to throw the fight. I guess he's afraid his son will get hurt before he can face the champ."

"But you wouldn't be bought."

"Hell, no. This is my chance to get back in the heavyweight picture. Did you know that I fought Mike McCoole twelve years ago for thirty rounds before he stopped me? And I wasn't even in shape."

"The old man's name wouldn't be Frank, would it?"

Sullivan shook his head emphatically and added, "Besides, he wouldn't do his own dirty work, anyway. He's a gentleman."

"Sure," Tracker said. "Has he got any other sons, or relatives named Frank?"

"Not that I know of."

"Is he the only man who's approached you about throwing the fight?"

"Only one I can recollect," Sullivan answered. "I know a lot of boys who have told me they're gonna bet against me, and would appreciate it if I lost, but that was just bar talk."

"Maybe. We can look into that later. I guess my first step is to go and talk to Mr. Barrow tomorrow."

"You gonna stick by me, Tracker?" Sullivan asked.

"I hired on as a sparring partner, didn't I?" Tracker replied. "I guess we'll just let Mr. Barrow know about that, too."

As much as Sullivan wanted Tracker as a sparring partner, he felt he had to warn him about Barrow.

"If those were Barrow's men who jumped you in the alley, and you tell him that, they might try to kill you next time."

"The key word there," Tracker pointed out, putting down his empty mug and picking up his hat, "is *try*. I'll see you in the morning, Will."

Sullivan smiled widely and said, "Good. I'll go with you to see Barrow and—"

"Not tomorrow, Will," Tracker told him. "I'll go and see Mr. Barrow alone. You're going to supervise the construction of a ring in the back storeroom of this hotel."

Sullivan's mouth dropped open and he stared at Tracker in total astonishment.

"How the hell did you arrange that?" he asked.

"Never mind," Tracker said. "Just be in that storeroom tomorrow morning and make sure everything is done right."

"You bet I will!" Sullivan replied eagerly. "You better damn well bet I will!"

Tracker laughed and patted Sullivan on his big shoulder.

"The minute I laid eyes on you, Tracker, I knew you were the right man for me!"

"Sure, Will," Tracker replied. "See you tomorrow."

When Tracker went back through the dining room he noticed that Deirdre Long had apparently finished her dinner and gone to her room. He wondered idly if he would have stopped to talk to her had she still been there.

Later, he thought, he could always talk to her later.

He went back to his suite, and as he opened his door he realized how tired he really was. Not just sleepy, but physically tired.

As he began to undress he became aware of another presence in the room. With his gun in one hand he turned up the lamp and saw that there was someone lying in his bed.

"Hey!" a woman's voice complained. "Douse the light, will you?"

The girl, Nora, stuck her head out from underneath the sheet and peered at him from beneath her tousled black hair.

"You're not gonna shoot me, are you?" she inquired.

"Not if you don't have any weapons under there with you," he told her.

In one quick motion she kicked the sheet off, revealing herself to be totally naked underneath.

"You see any weapons?" she asked.

Putting his gun away, he said, "None man-made, anyway."

She leaned back on her elbows and posed for him, breasts thrust forward, one leg bent. She knew how men liked to look at her, and she wanted this big man to be pleased by what he saw.

Tracker discovered that he wasn't at all as tired as he had thought he was.

42

Sometime during the night Nora lay in the crook of his arm and said, "The minute I laid eyes on you, Tracker, I knew you were the right man for me."

As he drifted off to sleep Tracker thought he had heard those words before.

Chapter 8

When Tracker and Nora woke the following morning, he sent her downstairs to find Farrell, and to have breakfast sent up to him. She had already told him that she wouldn't be able to stay and eat breakfast with him.

"Will I see you later?" she asked before leaving.

"That depends," Tracker said, not wanting to commit himself. He never wanted to commit himself, not when it came to women. There were too many around to do that. "We'll see."

Nora sighed and guessed that this was as much as she would be able to get out of him by way of a promise, and decided to be satisfied with it.

By the time Farrell showed up at his room—with his breakfast on a tray—Tracker had bathed and dressed.

"Here's your grub," Duke said as Tracker opened the door to his knock.

"Set it down anywhere, boy," Tracker said, and Duke made a face at him.

"This isn't going to help matters with Deirdre, you

44

know," he told Tracker. "She saw me bringing this up to you, and she's even more curious than ever."

"What'd you tell her last night?"

"I avoided her completely," Duke said. "What'd you want to see me so early about?"

"I want you to have some men meet Sullivan in the storeroom. They're to do whatever he tells them as far as building a boxing ring is concerned. Understand?"

Duke could tell by the look in his friend's eyes that there was no point in arguing with him, so he nodded and said, "Yeah, I got it. What are you going to be doing today?"

Tracker picked up a chunk of ham and popped it into his mouth, and poured a cup of coffee from the pot on the tray.

"Want one?" he asked Duke, and when the smaller man answered yes, he poured him a cup as well.

"I'm going to go and see a man named Barrow," he told Duke, handing him a cup.

"Lucas Barrow?" Duke asked, surprised.

"Is that his name?"

"Barrow's a powerful man, Tracker," Duke warned. "He's got friends in high places. What do you want to see him for?"

"I understand it's his son that Will Sullivan is supposed to fight."

"So?"

"I also understand that he tried to buy Will off. Failing that, I think he's passed the word that no one is to help Will get ready. That's why Will hasn't been able to find any sparring partners."

"I get it. You think that Barrow found out about you and sent some of his men to give you the message."

"Right."

"Walk careful around Barrow, Tracker," Duke warned. "He's a dangerous man."

"Have you ever seen the man I couldn't handle, Duke?" Tracker asked.

"That's true enough, but this isn't the open West," Duke informed the larger man. "This is the city, and things are done differently here."

"I'm not going to blow his head off, Duke," Tracker said. "I'm just going to talk to him, reason with him."

"And if that doesn't work?"

Tracker smiled and Duke shuddered when he saw it.

He didn't know who to feel sorrier for, Tracker or Barrow.

Knowing Tracker as well as he did, however, he knew who he would bet on.

Chapter 9

Tracker received instructions from Duke Farrell as to where to find Lucas Barrow, but Duke advised that he not try until sometime in the afternoon.

"You'll find him at his place, the Alhambra, then," Duke told him, "but in the morning nobody seems to know where he is. Instead of running around all morning, you might as well wait."

Tracker took his friend's advice, and unhurriedly finished his breakfast. Duke stayed in the room while his friend ate, and seemed to have something on his mind, but Tracker decided to let him bring it up on his own.

When Tracker was on his last cup of coffee, Duke finally spoke up.

"We have a small problem, Tracker, that you should know about," he said.

"We?" Tracker asked.

"The hotel," Duke clarified.

"Meaning you, me and Miss Long."

"Uh, right."

"Okay, Duke, it's been gnawing at you all morning, so spit it out. What's on your mind?"

"Accidents," Duke said.

Tracker stared at his friend, waiting for him to elaborate, and when he did not, he repeated, "Accidents? What kind of accidents?"

"Small ones," Duke said, "but an awful lot of them, Tracker. I don't think they're really accidents, either."

"Wait a minute," Tracker said, shaking his head as if to clear it. "You're confusing me, Duke. Where are these accidents happening?"

"Here in the hotel," Duke answered. "Little things, Tracker, but they pile up."

"You want to tell me what some of these little things are?" Tracker asked, getting a little annoyed because Duke wasn't being all that clear.

"Oh, shit, Tracker," Duke said, "I mean things like one of our cooks getting scalded with a pot of boiling water. The man's a pro, for Christ's sake, somebody had to have dumped it on him. Then the back outside staircase, it almost caved in under a couple of guests. I'm sure it was tampered with. We had to spend a lot of money to hire a new cook, and build a new staircase."

"So these 'accidents' are deliberate, and they're costing us money, right?" Tracker said.

"Right. That's what I'm telling you."

"And you can't figure it?"

"I could figure it if we had somebody trying to buy the hotel," Duke said. "I'm not a fool, Tracker, you know that, but we haven't had any offers."

"How long have these accidents been going on?"

"Since I got here."

"None before?"

"Not according to Deirdre," Duke answered.

"And no offers to buy before your arrival?"

Duke shook his head and answered, "None."

"Have you seen any of your, uh, old friends in town?" Tracker asked.

Duke Farrell had been in his business a long time, the business of "conning" people into thinking that they haven't been conned. He'd made his share of enemies over the years, as had Tracker, himself.

48

"None of my friends, Tracker," Duke answered, "or yours."

"Mine?" Tracker asked, frowning at his friend. "Why mine? Who knows about my connection to the hotel?"

"Nobody that I know of," Duke said, hurriedly. "I was just saying that I haven't seen anybody you or I know anywhere near here."

Tracker went over to the closet and began going through the wardrobe Duke had supplied him with. When he'd picked out a suit he wanted, he turned and dropped it on the bed.

"Hire a couple of guys to act as around-the-clock security," he told Duke, slipping on a clean shirt. "That's about all we can do until an offer is made."

"You really think there will be one?" Duke asked.

"I really think so," Tracker answered. "Once there is, and we say no, we'll see how they react. How would Miss Long react to the prospect of selling the place?"

Duke shook his head and said, "Dead set against it," in a positive tone.

"You sure?" Tracker asked, starting to put on the suit.

"I asked her about selling her share, already," Duke replied.

Tracker looked at the smaller man and asked, "For you, or for me?"

"Well, for you, of course. I didn't figure you'd want to split the place with a woman," Duke explained.

"Or anyone, for that matter," Tracker said, strapping on his gun. He knew how "the con" ran deep in Duke Farrell's blood, as necessary to his survival as the blood itself. Duke was not above conning a friend, although he'd never tried it with Tracker... yet.

To Duke, that would be the ultimate challenge—if he could work up the courage.

To Tracker, it would be the ultimate betrayal, and he hoped Duke would never try it.

Chapter 10

Portsmouth Square was the center of San Francisco's gambling community. Among the halls found there were the El Dorado, Bella Union, Parker House, Mazourka Arcade, Varsouvienne, Dennison's Exchange, Frontine House and the Alhambra. They all offered essentially the same things: free food on the bars, music, pretty women—some of whom were prostitutes, some of whom were there simply for "gawking privileges." Since the men outnumbered the women in San Francisco by ten to one, many customers were happy just to be able to come in and gawk at the pretty girls. The music was supplied by violinists, harpists and one-man bands. One such man plied his trade at the Verandah, with a drum on his back, drumsticks attached to his elbows and cymbals on his wrists.

Above all, however, all the saloons offered gambling in all of its forms. The most popular games were roulette, rondo, blackjack, faro and poker.

The only other section of the city that might have matched the Square were parts of Sacramento Street, and all of the eastern side of Dupont Street. This area was crowded with Chinese gambling halls, where dice and dominoes were offered, as well as the other forms of gambling.

Tracker waited until after two in the afternoon to go looking for Lucas Barrow. He spent most of his waiting time watching the progress that was being made erecting the boxing ring in the back storeroom.

He also spent time avoiding Deirdre Long, although he knew that wouldn't last. Sooner or later he would have to talk to her, and there were certain types of conversation he thought he might look forward to having with her. For now, however, he wanted to leave it to Duke to deal with her, until he decided whether or not he was going to let her in on the fact that he, not Duke Farrell, was her partner.

"How's it going?" he asked Will Sullivan.

"Fine," Sullivan said, jumping down from the raised ring apron. "I have to go behind the bar, but these boys can finish up the job." He mopped his broad brow and said, "I don't know how you arranged it, but I sure do appreciate it."

"Will a week's sparring be enough for you?" Tracker asked him.

"It'll have to be, won't it?" Sullivan replied. "Don't worry, friend," he said, dropping a heavy hand on Tracker's shoulder, "you'll get your money."

"I'm not all that worried about the money, Will," Tracker told the boxer. "I'd just like to see you win."

"Me, too, friend," Sullivan said. "Me, too."

Sullivan went to take up his position behind the bar, and Tracker started out for Portsmouth Square.

Tracker's hotel, Farrell House—and that would have to be changed sometime soon—was only about two blocks off the Square. Right now it did not offer much more gambling than pickup poker games, but once he'd made his decision about whether or not to reveal his connection, he could decide whether or not to add other forms of gambling. It was close enough to the Square to make a nice piece of change from the "overflow" of customers.

It was still early, but when Tracker hit the Square he found it teeming with activity. Gambling halls were side by side, and he had no doubt but that they were all taking in a fortune. If there was competition, it was for the sake of competition, or for reasons of pride. Nobody was going to put anyone else out of business. There were too many people willing to lose their money for that to ever happen.

Tracker located the Alhambra and was impressed. It was one of the classiest-looking halls on the Square. He crossed the Square and entered.

There was no pretense about what the Alhambra was. When you walked in you found yourself in a massive room, with crystal chandeliers and every type of gaming table you could think of. Off to the right was a bar that ran the length of the room. On the left there was an entranceway that apparently led to a dining room, but this was the main room, right here, where all of the action took place.

Tracker walked to the bar and ordered a whiskey. As he expected, he was served quality liquor, not the watered-down bar whiskey he was used to getting. He downed it, savored the exquisite bite and burn of it, and then ordered another.

"Good booze," he commented when the bartender gave him his second drink.

"That's all we serve, sir," the man told him haughtily. "The best."

"Yeah," Tracker replied, picking up the glass, "it figures."

He turned and leaned against the bar, drink in hand. Money was changing hands all over the place, most of it going to the house, in whose favor the odds always were. He expected that some of the games would be rigged, maybe not to cheat the customers, but surely to enable the house to break a hot player's streak by some artificial means.

He finished the second drink and decided against ordering a third. He didn't want to spoil himself. Instead, he turned to the bartender and asked, "Where's Mr. Barrow?"

The bartender regarded Tracker critically, obviously not impressed by the cut of his clothing, or the worn holster and .45 on his hip. *He can see that I don't belong*

52

in these clothes, Tracker thought, and maybe not even this town.

"I believe Mr. Barrow is lunching in the dining room, sir," the bartender told him.

"Thanks, friend," Tracker said, but the bartender elevated his nose and strolled down to the other end of the bar.

Tracker ignored the slight and headed for the entrance to the dining room. As he approached it a man appeared out of nowhere and barred his path.

He was an inch or so shorter than Tracker, but he weighed about the same. He was a good-sized man, dressed well, with a gun in a shoulder holster beneath his jacket. Tracker thought that he didn't look like he belonged there, either.

"Can I help you?" the man asked. He put his hand straight out and Tracker stopped just out of the man's reach.

"I'd like to see Mr. Lucas Barrow," Tracker replied.

The man shook his head and said, "Mr. Barrow don't like to be bothered while he's having lunch."

"I think he'll see me," Tracker said.

The other man smiled and asked, "Now what makes you say that, stranger?"

"Tell him my name is Tracker," he answered, "and that I'm Will Sullivan's sparring partner." Then, after a short pause, he added on impulse, "And manager."

Chapter 11

Lucas Barrow surprised his personal bodyguard, Dan Logan, and told him to bring "Mr. Tracker" to his table. He also instructed the waiter to set another place for lunch.

Logan, surprised at his boss's decision, went back to the door and gruffly told Tracker, "He'll see you. This way."

Tracker followed Logan to Barrow's special table, and as they approached Barrow stood up.

"Mr. Tracker. Welcome. Please join me for lunch, won't you?"

"Thanks," Tracker replied. Before seating himself he glanced sideways at the bodyguard, Logan. Barrow got the message.

"You can go back to the door, Dan," Barrow told the man.

"But boss—" Logan started to protest.

"It's all right, Dan. I don't think Mister Tracker came here to shoot me in plain sight of the other diners."

Logan looked annoyed, but he followed orders and went back to take up his position by the door.

"You didn't come here to shoot me, did you?" Barrow asked Tracker.

"No," Tracker answered, shortly.

Barrow was a lean man who was in his sixties, and wore the years well. He had a head of snow white hair and a full beard to match, and both hair and beard were professionally kept.

"Will you have a drink?" he asked.

"I could use a beer, thanks," Tracker replied.

"And of course you'll have something to eat. My chef does wonders with lamb—"

"Just the drink, Mr. Barrow," Tracker said, "and maybe some plain talk."

Barrow raised his eyebrows and sat back in his chair, studying Tracker for a moment. He was trying to decide what he was dealing with here. It was obvious that the clothing the man was wearing did not quite fit his personality. Was it possible that the big man was more intelligent than Barrow assumed?

"Very well, Mr. Tracker. What shall we talk plain about?" he finally asked.

"Let's talk about your son's match with Will Sullivan," Tracker suggested as a waiter brought his beer.

"Sullivan," Barrow repeated. "I must say I'm surprised to hear that you're managing him, now, as well as sparring with him."

"I understand you sewed the town up pretty tight, as far as Will getting anyone to help him get ready for the fight, so I can understand that you might be surprised. I intend to do the best I can to get Will into shape to beat your son, Mr. Barrow."

"Well, I guess that's only fair, isn't it?" Barrow answered. "Both men should be in the best shape possible, and I assure you, my son is."

"That's fine. Then we can have a nice, fair fight."

"I wouldn't have it any other way, Mr. Tracker. Now, as far as my sewing up the town against him, I don't know where—"

"Let me just say this, Mr. Barrow," Tracker said, standing up now, so Barrow would be forced to stare up at him. "I wouldn't take it too kindly if I caught someone tampering with my fighter."

"What do you mean by tampering?" Barrow asked. He held up his hand, but Tracker had seen Logan coming towards him out of the corner of his eye. Barrow's hand slowed Logan down, but the bodyguard kept walking towards Tracker, who continued to keep half an eye on him.

"Offering him money to throw the fight—"

"That's a lie!" Barrow snapped.

"Is it?"

"My boy doesn't need any help in taking care of that broken-down old wreck," the man replied.

Tracker put both hands on the table and leaned over Lucas Barrow, who shrank back as far as his chair would allow.

"I had a visit last night from three men who didn't want me to help Will Sullivan in any way. I was unprepared for that visit, Mr. Barrow," Tracker informed the older man, "but that won't happen again. The next man who comes anywhere near me or my fighter will end up dead."

Barrow stared at Tracker, expressionless for a long moment, and then he started to laugh.

"You're actually threatening me," Barrow said in disbelief. "You're a nobody in this town, Tracker. You've only just arrived. I practically own it—or this part of it, anyway. I can make just about anything I want happen."

"I'm impressed," Tracker replied, "but what I said still goes. My fighter is going to beat your fighter in the ring, fairly, with no interference."

Shaking his head, Barrow said, "You really think that old wreck can beat my boy?"

"So do you," Tracker said, "or you wouldn't have tried to buy him, or make it hard for him to train, and you wouldn't have sent three of your men to scare me off." Tracker stood straight up now and added, "I don't scare, Barrow. You haven't got anyone big enough to do the job."

That statement seemed to interest Barrow very much, and he shifted in his chair and allowed his eyes to settle on his bodyguard, Dan Logan.

"You agree with that, Logan?" he asked.

"Sir?" Logan asked.

"Do you think that I haven't got anyone big enough to do the job?" Barrow asked his bodyguard. "Never mind, don't answer that." He looked at Tracker and said, "This might be a fine opportunity to see what kind of a sparring partner you'll make."

Tracker turned his head to look straight at Dan Logan.

"Logan stands between you and the door, Mr. Tracker," Barrow said. "You've got to get past him to get out. If you make it," he added, "I just might hire you to spar with my boy."

"I said you didn't have anybody big enough," Tracker said, "and that includes your boy." Tracker had never seen Homer Barrow, but he thought the remark would bother the boy's father.

"You'd better concentrate on Logan first, Tracker," Barrow advised him.

"And what's to stop me from putting a hole in him?" Tracker asked.

"This is not the untamed West, Tracker," Barrow told him. "This is San Francisco. Our police department frowns on murder." He turned his attention to Dan Logan and said, "Dan, put your gun aside. I want this to be a fair fight, and I want you to show Mr. Tracker what Will Sullivan can look forward to when he steps into the ring with my son. Do you understand?"

"Yes, sir," Logan said. He pulled aside his jacket and removed his gun from his shoulder holster. He placed it on a nearby table, and then removed his jacket. Tracker couldn't read the man's face. Beyond the fact that Logan seemed determined, he couldn't tell if there would be any enjoyment in it for the big man.

"I don't want to fight you, Logan," Tracker told him. "Just step aside and let me pass."

"I can't do that, Tracker," the bodyguard replied. Just a flat statement of fact with still no hint of what the man might have been feeling.

"I'll have to go through you, then," Tracker said.

Logan flexed his arms and said, "Nothing personal."

Tracker shook his head and started forward. He'd studied the man and knew this wouldn't be easy. As he'd noticed before, Logan was nearly his size, and on top of that he was about eight or nine years younger.

For most of his life, Tracker had settled arguments with his fists, not his gun. He was not a gunman, but more of a brawler. He had the feeling that Dan Logan was more of a gunman than a fighter, but there would only be one way to find out for sure.

He made as if he were going to walk right past Logan, who grabbed his arm to stop him, thus confirming what Tracker had suspected. If the man had been a fighter, he would have known to strike the first blow. Tracker allowed Logan to turn him around and brought his left fist crashing into the man's face. Logan, caught by surprise, staggered back and fell atop the table where he'd set his gun. Both table and man crashed to the floor, the table falling apart beneath his weight.

"Stay down, Logan," Tracker advised the younger man, but his words fell on deaf ears.

The young bodyguard pulled himself to his feet and wiped the blood from his mouth with the back of his hand. Tracker set himself. He expected the man to come at him swinging, but instead Logan lowered his head and bulled into Tracker, lifting him off his feet. Tracker found himself literally thrown atop a table, which also crumbled beneath his weight, sending him crashing to the floor.

"Get up," Logan told him, standing over him.

Tracker hooked one of Logan's ankles with his two feet and twisted, throwing the bodyguard off balance, but not knocking him off his feet, as he'd intended. Still, Tracker had time to get back on his own feet before Logan regained his balance.

Now the two big men faced each other, each having tested the other. Barrow sat back in his chair, watching intently, and several waiters had backed away as far as they could while still being able to watch.

Logan threw a long, looping right and Tracker stepped inside of the arc and struck a short left to the man's midsection. Logan grunted, but his stomach was all hard ridges and the blow failed to have the desired effect of folding the man up. Momentarily surprised at the lack of effectiveness of his hard punch, Tracker got careless and Logan threw a left of his own, catching

Tracker on the point of the chin. Tracker staggered back, spots forming before his eyes, but through the spots he could see Logan moving in to follow up his advantage. The bodyguard threw another left which Tracker was just quick enough to catch on his right forearm. He threw a left at Logan's face, but the man jerked his head back, minimizing the impact of the blow. Still, having been hit, he backed away for a moment, and that proved to be his undoing. Tracker's experience came into play as he decided to try to end the thing as quickly as possible. While Logan was trying to decide what to throw next, Tracker stepped in and faked with a left. Logan reacted by raising his right to block, and dropping his left. Tracker then threw his right hand instead of his left and hit Logan right where he wanted to, over the heart. The force of the punch, combined with its location, stunned Logan. He felt as if his heart had stopped and he couldn't seem to move his arms. Tracker threw another vicious right, catching Logan high on the cheek, and then threw a left hand, hitting the bodyguard just under his belt, avoiding the hard muscles he'd encountered before. He heard the air go out of Logan's lungs as his fist sank into a satisfying depth. He felt the young bodyguard begin to fold up, fighting for breath. He stepped away to allow Logan to fall to the floor. He waited a few moments, to see if the man would be able to rise, but when it became apparent he could not, he turned to face Barrow, who looked shocked.

"Remember what I said, Barrow," Tracker told him. "Keep your boy away from me and my fighter. In fact, I don't want them anywhere near the Farrell House hotel, where Sullivan works, and where I'm staying. Do yourself a favor. Spend the rest of the time until the fight getting your boy into shape."

"He'll be in shape, Tracker," Barrow said. "Your fighter is going to get his," he added, "just like you're going to get yours if you stay in San Francisco."

Tracker stepped over the fallen figure of Dan Logan, who was still gasping for air, and on his way to the door called out, "I hope your boy is better than your bodyguard."

Barrow watched Tracker's retreating back until he

was out of the room, and then he looked down at his bodyguard, who was just pushing himself up off the floor.

"Logan, you've got one last chance," he informed the man as he staggered to his feet, holding one hand to his chest. "If that man isn't dead by the end of the week," Barrow told his bodyguard, "you sure as hell will be!"

Chapter 12

"You can't hold back," Will Sullivan told him. "You've got to give me all you've got, or it won't do me any good. Okay?"

Facing Will Sullivan across the newly erected ring, Tracker nodded and said, "Okay. Let's go."

Sullivan signaled Duke Farrell, who was acting as timekeeper, and Duke struck a bell, signaling the start of the first round of sparring.

Tracker was impressed with Will Sullivan's condition. The man seemed to be chiseled from stone. His chest muscles were like two hard slabs, his shoulders padded with thick muscles and covered with dark hair that almost resembled fur.

In spite of what Sullivan had told him about giving his all, Tracker couldn't help but hold back a little. Will's face was covered with scar tissue, a decent shot could open up a cut and jeopardize the fight. Also, the telltale gray in the old fighter's hair reminded Tracker that the man was at least ten years older than he, and probably more.

After three rounds, Tracker's face stung from the shots he'd taken from Sullivan's rock-hard fists. The boxer seemed to be strictly a headhunter, and he didn't pay too much attention to defense, but he could hit hard, that much was for sure.

"Come on, Tracker," he shouted from across the ring, "you're holding back."

"Yeah," Tracker said to himself. His breath was starting to come in ragged gasps, and his lungs were burning. He'd considered himself to be in pretty good shape, but this was making him realize that he'd been kidding himself. Too many sessions at the poker table, and too much food and drink.

As round four started he decided to test Sullivan's body. He threw a couple of rights into the other man's stomach, and found what he thought might be his only weakness. Age had taken some of the firmness out of Sullivan's belly, and he wouldn't be able to take too much body punishment if the fight went long. He was going to have to have Will work on his stomach during the week they had left.

As the round was coming to a close Sullivan stepped into a Tracker right-hand. He staggered back a step or two, shook his head and for a moment Tracker thought his eyes went out of focus. As Duke signaled the end of the round Tracker approached Sullivan with his hands out, to steady him. Sullivan had apparently not heard the end of the round and he threw a vicious right that would have taken Tracker's head off had he not ducked under it.

"Whoa, easy, Will!" he shouted. "The round is over!"

"What—" Sullivan started to say, as if he hadn't understood.

"End of the round," Tracker said again, softer.

Sullivan looked into Tracker's face and his expression seemed to change. He seemed aware again.

"Sorry, kid," he said, patting Tracker on the shoulder. "Sorry."

"Sure, forget it," Tracker told him. "The heat of battle and all."

"You were still holding back, Kid," Sullivan said as they stepped through the ropes to the outside of the ring.

62

"You don't fool me, Will," Tracker replied. "You were holding back, too."

"What are you talking about?" Sullivan asked. "You took some good shots in there, Tracker."

"Yeah?" Tracker said. "Well, you need some work on your belly, friend," he informed Sullivan, patting the man's stomach. "My fist goes in there much too deep. Got to harden that up by fight time."

Sullivan frowned and touched his stomach.

"Really?"

"Really. You going to tell me you didn't feel those belly punches?"

Rubbing his belly in a circular motion, Sullivan admitted, "I guess maybe you're right."

"Sure I'm right. Stop drinking the hotel's beer while you're tending bar, huh?"

"Sure, Tracker, sure."

As they toweled off Tracker said, "Are you okay?"

"Sure, why?"

"That last right hand seemd to rock you a little," Tracker said.

Sullivan laughed and said, "Oh, you think so, huh? Well, you'll get another chance tomorrow to test your right hand on this old head."

"Sure."

Sullivan dropped his towel and started to leave, but Tracker called out to him.

"Will!"

"Yeah, kid?"

"I went to see Lucus Barrow today."

"Hey, that's right," Sullivan replied, walking back to face Tracker. "What happened?"

"I told him I was your sparring partner—and your manager. I hope you don't mind."

Sullivan shook his head and said, "Naw, I don't mind, long as you ain't looking for a manager's cut of the purse."

"Don't worry about that. I warned Barrow off, and he set his bodyguard on me."

"Dan Logan?" Sullivan replied. "He's a big man, Logan is. That where you got that bruise on your chin?"

"That's where."

"I wish I was there to see that. What happened?"

63

"Let's just say Logan was having a little trouble catching his breath when I left."

"You took Logan, huh?" Sullivan asked, obviously impressed. "He's young and strong."

"No experience, though," Tracker said.

"Maybe not, but at least that tells me one thing for sure," Sullivan observed.

"What's that?"

Flicking a thumb at the ring, Sullivan said, "You sure as hell were holding back in there. Tomorrow I expect you to give me some of what you gave Dan Logan. Okay?"

"Sure, Will. Sure. I'll see you later."

"Okay, kid."

"And lay off the beer," Tracker called after him as he left.

When Sullivan was gone, Duke came over to stand next to Tracker.

"What happened in there?" he asked.

"I don't know," Tracker said, still watching the door that Will Sullivan had gone through. "I didn't hit him that hard, but he seemed to forget where he was."

"He almost took your head off, too. I think you're crazy getting mixed up with him."

"Nobody asked you what you think, Duke," Tracker said absently.

"Okay," Duke said. "Okay."

Tracker looked at his friend, then clapped him on the shoulder to soften the effect of his remark and asked, "How are you doing with Miss Long?"

"She's getting harder and harder to put off, Tracker," Duke answered. "I think you should tell her."

"Why?"

"Well, we got these accidents going, and now you're mixed up with Barrow. If things start to get sticky, she should know this place is yours, otherwise she might get in the way with her questions," Duke replied.

"You might be right," Tracker conceded. "Let me think about it. If I decide to tell her, I'll let you know."

"Sure, Tracker."

"Any more accidents?"

"No, not yet."

"And no prospective buyers, nobody looking us over?"

"Nope."

"Okay. I'm going to take a bath. I'll see you later."

"Okay, but I still think you're crazy to get mixed up with some old fighter's dream of one more shot at the top."

Tracker felt the sore spots on his face from Sullivan's hands and wondered if his friend might not be right. Then he remembered the smug superiority on Lucas Barrow's face and decided that Duke wasn't right after all.

Tracker hoped that Lucas Barrow would have a nice front row seat, so Sullivan could deposit his son right in his lap.

Chapter 13

Tracker stepped naked and dripping wet from the private bathtub in his suite, walked into the main room that way and almost walked right into Deirdre Long.

"Well, hello," he said, regarding her without any trace of embarrassment. To her credit, she managed to appear totally unaffected by the situation as well, although deep down she was impressed by what she saw. She saw a tall man, broad shouldered, slim hipped and, uh, well endowed, and she kept her face blank while she admired these attributes.

Deirdre Long was not the innocent little girl Duke Farrell and some other people seemed to think she was. Before she and her father "lucked" into the hotel business, they had traveled all over the West, working every kind of job, every kind of "con" imaginable. This hotel was a chance at running a legitimate business and, until her father died, they were doing a pretty good job. Now she found out that her father had either sold or lost half-interest in the hotel, and whoever the other owner was he had lost it to Duke Farrell, who seemed intent on changing things in the hotel. She'd been trying to figure Farrell's angle ever since his arrival, and now she was further confused by the appearance of this man, Tracker. Duke Farrell had repeatedly put her off when she asked about Tracker, so she decided to go to the man himself for some answers.

As part owner of the hotel, she naturally had access to every one of its rooms. She used a key to get into Tracker's suite and was trying to decide whether or not she should wait for him to return when he surprised her and walked out of the bathroom, fresh from the bath.

"Very impressive," she replied to his greeting, hiding both her surprise at his appearance and the fact that she was impressed by his physique.

"Are you here to steal something," he asked, "or to check and see if I have?"

"I'm here for some answers, Mr. Tracker," she said. "I haven't been able to get any from your evasive little friend, so I thought I might have better luck with you."

"Would you mind if I put something on first?" he asked, studying her closely.

"Not at all," she replied. "In fact, I'd prefer it."

Tracker wasn't at all sure that was true, but he proceeded to get dressed while Deirdre Long stood by, still totally unembarrassed. He was puzzled by the fact that she had not even come close to blushing. If she was the sweet young lady that Duke Farrell had made her out to be—stubborn, and determined, but still a lady— then her reaction here was very odd, indeed.

The first time he had met her he had been flat on his back and probably not yet fully conscious, so he had not had an opprotunity to really look at her then. He took that opportunity now, and was impressed by what he saw. She appeared to be about twenty-four with long, shimmering blond hair, blue eyes, a lovely cupid's bow mouth, and full breasts and hips. Once again she was wearing a high-necked, chaste dress that didn't quite fit what little Tracker knew of her personality.

She just didn't strike Tracker as the "chaste" type.

When he was fully dressed he strapped on his gun and said to her, "Can we go someplace and talk?"

"You mean, you're willing to talk to me?" she asked,

and this time her surprise was apparent. She had obviously expected him to try to evade her questions and brush her aside the way Duke Farrell had been doing.

"Of course," he replied. "I'd be a fool not to want to talk to a lovely woman."

Deirdre looked at him strangely for a few moments, and then she said, "Oh, no you don't. Your friend Farrell has been very nicely sidestepping the issues, and now you're going to try to sweet-talk your way past me? It's not going to work, Mr. Tracker," she said, sitting herself down firmly on his bed. "We're going to stay right here and talk this thing out. I want some straight answers, for a change."

"What about your honor?" he asked. "What are the other guests going to say about you being in my room—"

"Cut the crap, Tracker!" she snapped.

He looked shocked and said, "That's no way for a lady to talk."

"The hell with being a lady. I want some answers!"

"Okay, okay," he said, holding up his hands in a gesture of surrender. "What are the questions."

"Who are you, who is Farrell, and why is he letting you turn my hotel into a boxing ring."

"Our hotel, Miss Long," he replied, and that stopped her for a moment.

"Our hotel?" she asked him. "You mean, you have a piece of it, too, as well as Duke Farrell?" She put her hands on her hips and said disgustedly, "Just how many goddamn pieces is this place sliced up into?"

"Just two, Miss Long," Tracker answered. "Just two, yours and mine."

"You mean, Farrell—"

"Duke was just acting for me, until I could decide whether or not I wanted to get into the hotel business," he explained.

"Oh, I see," she said. She looked down and studied the back of her hand while she examined her feelings about this new turn of events.

"So, you're my partner, not Farrell," she finally said.

"That's right."

"And now you've decided that you want to get into the hotel business?"

He looked very deliberately at her, smiled and said, "Well, the prospect does seem to get better and better all the time."

"You're doing it again," she said reproachfully.

"What?"

"Trying to sweet-talk your way around me."

"Sorry."

"Why have you suddenly decided that you might like the hotel business?" she asked, and then added, "without the horseshit, please."

"Several reasons," he said, "and we can discuss them another time. Right now we have one irrefutable fact, and that is that we are partners."

"So?"

"So, Duke tells me that we've been having some problems with accidents."

"Oh, that," she said. "That's all they are, accidents."

"Not according to Duke, and I usually trust his instincts," he told her.

"Does he work for you?"

"Not exactly," he answered. "We're, uh...friends, I guess you could say. We've known each other a long time."

"And he doesn't think that these incidents have been accidental?" she asked.

"No, he doesn't."

"Does he say why?"

"He doesn't know why, Deirdre—uh, can I call you Deirdre? We are partners, you know."

"There's still the little matter of showing me a piece of paper," she pointed out, "but sure, call me what you like. What do I call you?"

"What everybody else does," he answered. "Tracker."

She waited a few seconds, and when no further name was forthcoming, she said, "All right, *Tracker*, why would somebody be causing accidents in my—um, in *our* hotel?"

"We don't know, Deirdre," he answered, "but I have the feeling that very shortly we will be getting an offer to buy the place."

She laughed.

"With all the big places down the block in Portsmouth Square, who'd want to buy this one?"

He smiled and said, "Somebody who knows how to make accidents happen on purpose."

"You seriously think somebody wants this place?" she asked.

"You've never been approached by someone who might have wanted to buy it?" Tracker asked.

"No, no one," she replied.

"Not even Duke Farrell?"

She frowned at him and said, "Well, that was different. He just wanted to know if I would sell my forty-nine percent share."

"To who?"

"Uh, I assumed he meant to him—that is, to you, since he was acting for you, wasn't he?"

"I hope so," Tracker replied.

"Look, I'd like to talk about what's going on in the storeroom," she said, changing the subject.

"I'm helping a fighter get into shape for a fight, that's all," he explained.

"Do you own a piece of the fighter?" she asked.

"Not really," he said, then he thought again. "Actually, maybe we both own a piece of him."

"What do you mean?"

"He works for us, in the saloon. He's a bartender. His name is Will Sullivan."

"Sullivan?" she said, frowning. "I don't remember any—he must have been hired by your friend, Farrell."

Duke hadn't mentioned that, but then again, why should he have? Tracker hadn't actually asked him what changes if any he'd made in the operation of the hotel. Aside from the name change, he must have hired or fired some new help.

"Are you going to make some changes in the hotel operation now?" she asked him.

"I haven't decided," he answered. "I'd like to settle the matters of the accidents and the fight before I start thinking about that."

"Well, what about Farrell? What's he going to be doing?"

"He's going to continue to act for me," Tracker said. "I want to stay behind the scenes."

"For how long?" she asked.

"Maybe for as long as I own a piece of the hotel," he

70

said. "I haven't decided about that, either. You know, you ask more questions than any woman I ever knew."

"Is that so? And how many women have you known?"

"Enough," he assured her.

"I'll bet." She stood up and said, "Well, I guess I should be grateful that you've answered most of my questions. Some other time I guess we could talk about what makes you think you can run a hotel."

"Oh, I didn't say anything about running it," he told her. "I simply said that I own it."

"Half of it," she reminded him.

"Fifty-one percent of it," he corrected her.

She stared at him hard and said, "I think maybe I didn't know when I was well off."

"What's that supposed to mean?"

"I think I should have been satisfied with Duke Farrell as a partner and let it go at that!"

It was amazing, but when she got angry her blue eyes seemed to become an even deeper blue, and the added color that flooded her face seemed to make her lovely face glow.

"Hold it," Tracker said, holding his hands up. "Truce. Why don't we go downstairs and have a nice dinner, and we can finish this discussion without raising our voices. I think since we are partners now, we should try and learn to get along. What do you say?"

She took a moment to overcome her temper, doing so by taking several deep breaths which Tracker enjoyed immensely.

"All right," she agreed. "We'll meet downstairs in an hour."

"An hour?"

"Well, I have to get ready, you know," she told him.

"Okay, an hour," he agreed.

She walked to the door and, with her hand on the knob, turned back to him again.

"Oh, and Mr. Tracker?" she called out.

"Yes?"

"Please don't forget that important piece of paper. I'd like to be sure that we're partners before I start acting like one."

71

"All right, Miss Long," he replied, "but I'm sure you'll bring yours along, also, just so we're each sure of where we stand?"

"In an hour," she said and left.

Chapter 14

Dan Logan watched Homer Barrow spar with a shorter, lighter man and was impressed by the kid's hand speed. By rights, the smaller man should have been faster, but Barrow was holding his own, picking off the smaller man's punches, and then banging the other man's body. After a few body shots, the other man dropped his hands, and the kid nailed him with a hard right that sent him to the floor.

"Time!" the kid's trainer called, and Homer walked away from the smaller man without offering to help him up.

"Kid, I keep telling you," his trainer scolded him, "if you're gonna kill your sparring partners, you're not gonna have any more!"

"I don't need no more," the kid answered. "I'm ready for Will Sullivan now."

"Yeah, sure," the trainer replied. "Go get cleaned up, okay? Your old man's waiting for you to have dinner with him."

Homer spotted Logan and said, "Hey, Danny." He

walked over and patted the bodyguard on the back. "How you doing?"

"Fine, just fine," Logan told him. He didn't like the kid, but Mr. Barrow had told him to become friends with him, so he did his best to hide his feelings.

"What happened to your face?" the kid asked.

Logan's hand quickly went up to the bruise left by Tracker's fist and said, "Nothing. Traded bruises with a guy. Why don't you go and get cleaned up, and then we'll go see your father?"

"Sure, Danny, sure. I'd like to get a look at the other guy, huh?" Homer said, patting Logan on the back again.

"Sure, Homer, sure."

The kid's face froze and he said, "Aw geez, Danny, I've asked you not to call me Homer. I hate that friggin' name."

"Okay, kid, okay," Logan told him, smiling inside as he always did when he called the kid by his proper name. "Go ahead, I'll wait for you here."

He watched as Homer walked away, a tall, heavily muscled kid with no waist to speak of. The same could be said of his brain. Still, he could fight. Logan knew because he was the kid's first sparring partner, and he soon quit that job. The kid could hit hard and hurt you without knowing it—and at twenty he didn't even have his full growth yet.

Still, personality-wise, the kid was a shit.

The kid's trainer came over, a slim, medium-sized man who had been training fighters for years, without ever having a champion. He had dark hair that was going gray and a short, brush mustache that was even grayer.

"How does he look, Parker?" Logan asked.

The trainer squinted at him and said, "The old man send you to check on him, or me?"

"Relax. He wants the kid to have dinner with him, that's all."

"That's all? For that he sends his bodyguard?" Parker noticed the bruise on Logan's face and said, "What happened to you?"

Logan touched the bruise and said, "That guy Tracker came to see Mr. Barrow."

"Yeah? He's still around, huh? What'd he want?"

74

"He wanted to tell the boss that he's not only going to spar with that old fighter, he's gonna manage him, too."

"And then you and him went at it, huh?"

"Yeah," Logan muttered and then rushed on. "Listen, the boss wants this guy dead before the fight, or I'm dead. If he ain't dead by then, the last thing I do on this earth is gonna be to kill you. You got it?"

"Yeah, sure, Danny, I got it," the trainer replied.

"You get the boys to go after him again, and this time finish him off."

"What about you?"

"If the boys can't handle it, then I'll do it," Logan said, touching his gun, "with this."

"Barrow put you in decent clothes and gave you a new gun with a fancy shoulder holster," the trainer said, "but you're still a gunfighter, huh?"

Logan poked the smaller man in the chest with his forefinger and said, "Don't you forget it, Parker. And another thing."

"What?"

"Lay low for a while."

"What for?"

"Tracker's looking for a guy named Frank. Seems he heard the name last night when the boys jumped him."

"Shit," Frank Parker said. "I told those morons not to use my name."

"Yeah, well, those morons better do the job right, this time," Logan told him, "or both you and me are gonna end up dead, understand?"

"Yeah, sure," Parker said.

"Go and hurry Homer up, will you?" Logan told him.

"C'mon, Danny, don't call him that. You know it upsets him," Parker pleaded.

"Yeah," Logan said, smiling, "I know."

"You know," Parker said, watching the sparring partner finally drag himself from the ring, "I don't know why Barrow had to go looking for trouble, trying to keep Sullivan from getting into shape. The kid can take him."

"He can, huh?" Logan asked.

"Sure he can, especially with me training him," Frank Parker added.

"So you think Mr. Barrow is taking unnecessary precautions," Logan concluded.

"Uh, yeah, I think so."

Logan poked Parker in the chest again and said, "So why don't you tell him?"

Parker stared into Logan's eyes for a few seconds, then looked away and stammered, "I, uh, better go and, uh, hurry the kid up."

Chapter 15

When Tracker told the waiter in the dining room that he was meeting Miss Long for dinner, the waiter showed him to "Miss Long's" table. He was sitting there for a half an hour and two beers before she showed up.

It was worth the wait.

She had changed into a long gown of shimmering pink satin, cut low to reveal the tops of her round, white breasts. There was a touch of rouge on her cheeks and her lips, and she looked stunning. All of the other male diners in the room turned their heads and followed her to her table, where Tracker rose, but a waiter beat him to the punch and held her chair for her.

"Thank you, Carlo," she said, and the waiter bowed and waited for instructions.

"Just bring me a drink for now, Carlo. We'll order dinner in a while."

"Very well, Miss," the waiter answered, and he walked off.

"Well," Tracker said, "you certainly came loaded for bear, didn't you?"

"What do you mean?" she asked innocently.

"Well, you obviously intend to dazzle me with your beauty, which I have to admit you have done. You look beautiful!"

"Thank you," she replied, pleased with the compliment but trying not to show it.

"But I think you're trying to do the same thing to me that you claim I was trying to do to you," Tracker said.

"What?"

"You said I was trying to sweet-talk you. I think you're trying the same thing, but in a different way."

"That's silly," she replied. "I just enjoy dressing for dinner."

"Is that so?" he said, remembering that she hadn't been so dressed when he'd seen her having dinner the night before.

"Yes, that is so. Did you bring that little piece of paper along with you?" she asked.

"I did, yes," he said. He took it from his inside jacket pocket and she extended her hand across the table.

"What about yours?" he asked.

She hesitated a moment, then removed hers from her bag, and they exchanged.

Tracker read the paper through, and it was just as Duke had said. Rhodes had specified that Deirdre Long would always own forty-nine percent of the hotel as long as he was the owner of the other fifty-one percent. There was no indication on the paper that any money had changed hands.

"This is my father's signature, all right," Deirdre said, refolding the paper and handing it back to Tracker. "I guess we really are partners."

Tracker hesitated now, still looking at her paper, but then he refolded it and said, "Yeah, I guess so, so why don't we start acting like partners?"

"And how do you suggest we do that?" she asked.

"Let's start thinking about what's best for the hotel," he suggested.

"That's all I've ever done," she replied. "Ever since my father and I opened the place."

"Well, good. Then we're agreed."

"That we have to think about what's best for the

hotel, yes," she said, "but I'm not so sure having a boxer train in our storeroom is for the good of the hotel."

"Why not? He's out of sight, he's not bothering the guests."

"I suppose—"

"And what if he does go on to become champ?" Tracker asked. "That would be great publicity for the hotel. I'm sure you'd like it if business got better."

"Well, of course I would."

"Good, then that's settled."

"No, it's not settled," she said, "but I'll go along with it—for now."

"All right. Now we can go on to our other problem."

"The accidents," she said.

"Right. I still think that we're being set up for an offer to buy. Somebody wants to make us—or the owners, since they don't know about me—eager to dump this place for a cheap price."

"Well, I'm not selling, no matter what," she replied stubbornly.

"No," he said, admiring her stubbornness now he knew that she was really his partner—in a way, "I don't suppose you would."

"My father built this place so we could be le—uh, so we could set down roots. He died here, and I'm not selling."

He waited a couple of moments, and then said, "So, okay. We won't sell."

"Well, you can sell if you want to—," she started.

"I don't want to," he said, cutting her off. "I think I'm going to like the hotel business. Shall we order dinner?"

She looked at him with a puzzled frown and then said, "Yes, why don't we?"

Chapter 16

Later, Tracker admitted to himself that he'd had his hopes, but the last thing Deirdre Long expected was to end up in bed with Tracker by the end of the evening. When it happened, however, it seemed very natural.

After dinner, Tracker walked Deirdre to her room on the second floor of the hotel, carrying what was left of the second bottle of wine they'd shared.

"I would invite you in for a drink," she told him, "but I don't have anything."

"We have this," he said, holding up the remnants of their second bottle.

She smiled and said, "All right. I'm pretty sure I have a couple of glasses."

They went into her room and finished what wine there was left, and then he said, "I suppose I ought to be going. I've got to spar with Will in the morning."

"Is that where you got those bruises on your face?" she asked, reaching up and touching him.

"Uh, yeah, there and, uh—yeah, that's where I got them," he replied, taking her hand in his.

They stood there like that for a few moments, and he studied her face for the umpteenth time that evening, liking very much what he saw.

"Um," she said, pulling her hand away gently, "I guess you should be going."

"Yes, I guess so," he agreed. "Good night."

"Good night," she replied.

He bent over, as if to give her a chaste good-night kiss, and she raised her chin to offer her face, but the kiss that followed was anything but innocent.

Her mouth opened willingly beneath his, to the surprise of both of them. Tracker encircled her waist with both of his hands and pulled her closer to him. Tentatively, her arms began to work their way around him, and then they were rubbing against each other while their mouths worked together avidly.

When they broke the kiss she said breathlessly, "This is silly. I'm not even sure yet that I don't dislike you."

"Maybe this will help you decide," he replied.

They kissed again, and then began to work at each other's clothing. When they were both naked they rubbed against each other again, and their bodies felt as if they were on fire.

He felt the pebble hardness of her nipples scraping at his skin, and she felt the throbbing readiness of his manhood between them.

"The bed," she whispered, "the bed."

She began to back towards her bed and he followed. When the back of her knees touched the mattress she sank down onto her back, and Tracker lay beside her.

As he began to kiss the soft flesh of her breasts and lick her kernel-hard nipples, she took hold of his head and said, "Oh, God, it's been such a long time."

Her hands eagerly sought the column of flesh between his legs and she felt a thrill when she took hold of it and found it so long and hard.

While her hands centered on that part of his body Tracker's large hands roamed over every inch of hers. He squeezed one breast in each hand and alternately bit her nipples. While she continued to work on him with her hands, he ran one hand down her body until it nestled between her legs, finding her moist and ready. When he inserted one finger inside her she bucked her hips and cried out, "No more, Tracker, no more playing. I'm ready!"

Since it was their first time, Tracker decided not to make her wait. Besides, he wanted it just as much as she did.

He raised himself above her and allowed her eager hands to guide him home. As he entered her moist, hot tunnel she cried out and moved her hands so that she could grasp his buttocks. They worked together until they found a rhythm that suited them both, and then they set about giving and taking as much pleasure as they could from each other.

Later she began to laugh softly as they lay side by side, and he asked her what was so funny.

"Us," she replied. "I was just thinking that now we're partners in more ways than one."

"Are you sorry?" he asked.

"Oh, of course not, Tracker," she said. "I just never thought we'd come to this when I first met you."

"Well, I have to admit, I thought about it once or twice, myself," he said.

"Well, I suppose I should be flattered."

"I don't think you flatter, or embarrass, very easily," Tracker said.

"What do you mean by that?" she asked from out of the darkness.

"You've got Duke Farrell convinced that you're this very nice, proper, stubborn young woman who wants the hotel to be very high class."

"And you don't think I'm nice?" she asked.

"Ah, trying to put me on the defensive," he observed. "I have a feeling you're as much a con woman as Duke is a con man."

"Duke's a con man?" she asked, sounding surprised.

"Born and bred. He's worked every kind of con there is to work, and then thought some up."

"I thought he was just a hotel man—"

"See? He convinced you, just as you convinced him. However, I don't think either one of you will ever be able to convince me of anything."

"You see through us both, huh?" she asked.

"Why don't you tell me about your background,

82

Deirdre? What did you do before you and your father built this place?"

She hesitated a moment and he waited for her voice to come out from the dark.

"We worked just about every kind of con there was to work," she finally answered, "and then we thought some up."

Chapter 17

"Her father was who?" Duke Farrell asked the following morning.

"Fred Long, better known in your circles as Frenchie Longo," Tracker explained again.

"Frenchie Longo?" Duke repeated. "I can't believe this. She's Frenchie Longo's kid?" Duke walked around Tracker's suite, shaking his head. "You know, I met her once when she was just about knee high." He gave Tracker a sheepish look and added, "I was kind of young myself, you know? But that was the only time I ever met big Frenchie Longo. After that I just heard about him. Jesus, I can't believe this," he said, shaking his head again.

"You're going to shake your head right off, Duke. Sit down and take it easy."

"Me," Duke said, sitting down, "she actually fooled me into thinking she was a nice, proper—"

"If it's any consolation to you, Duke," Tracker said, "you fooled her, too."

Duke brightened and asked, "I did?"

"Yeah, you did. She thought you were just a hotel guy who had funny ideas about how to run a hotel."

Duke frowned and said, "They weren't so funny—," but then he stopped and brightened again, saying, "I fooled big Frenchie's kid, huh?"

"I guess that makes both of you pretty good, huh?" Tracker asked.

"Well, she had a small advantage, you know," Duke said. "She learned from the best. Me, I learned the hard way, by doing it until I got it right—and believe me, I took some hard knocks until I did finally get it right."

"I know all about your hard knocks, Duke," Tracker reminded him. "Let's relax for a while, huh?"

Duke took a deep breath and said, "Okay, I'm relaxed. Now what?"

"Well, at least now we know we're all on the same side."

"Same side?" Duke said. "We're the same kind."

"Yeah, well, considering some of the things you and I have done, that's not paying the lady too much of a compliment, you know?" Tracker pointed out.

"Yeah, well, if she's Frenchie's daughter, she's done her share, too."

"That may be so."

"What the hell was Frenchie doing with this place?" Duke wondered aloud.

"Going straight," Tracker answered. "They had saved up their money and decided to build this place and start a legitimate business."

"Frenchie? I find that hard to believe."

"Well, he was getting old, Duke. When you run a con, you've got to be ready to move fast, and he just couldn't do it anymore."

"I guess we all got to get old, huh?" Duke asked. He was past forty himself, but he'd never really thought about what he would do if he got too old for his line of work.

"All right, let's not start thinking about it now, Duke," Tracker said. "I don't want you getting all depressed."

"Okay, so now Deirdre and I are out in the open. Did she ask you what you do?" Duke asked.

"I didn't give her a chance."

"What are you going to tell her?"

85

"What do I tell anyone?" Tracker asked.

"That's easy," Duke answered. "Nothing. I'm not even sure what you do."

"I play a little cards, travel a lot—"

"—and I've seen you kill a few people," Duke pointed out.

"Only when the situation called for it," Tracker said, making his own point. "I've never broken the law."

"I've seen you bend it on occasion," his friend said, "and I've seen you take it into your own hands, but no, I guess I can't say that I've ever seen you break it." Then Duke smiled and said, "I guess that's my department."

"Well, as far as all of the things that I've done, we can add sparring partner to the list," Tracker said, getting up. "I have to meet Will in the storeroom."

"What'd Deirdre say about that?" Duke asked, also standing up.

"I pointed out the obvious advantages of the situation, and she decided not to fight us on it."

"That's good. I guess we've got enough fights to worry about."

"We?" Tracker asked.

"Well, if you really think that Will Sullivan has a chance with your help, he's got that much of a better chance if I help, too, right?"

Tracker looked at his friend for a moment, then smiled and said, "With the two of us helping him, he's just about unbeatable."

Duke beamed at him, and Tracker said, "Yeah, come on, maybe I'll let you spar with him."

Duke's mouth fell open, and when Tracker left the room, he ran out after him, trying to rephrase his offer of assistance.

Chapter 18

"...and keep your left up," Duke told Tracker.

"If you tell me that again, Duke, I will send you in there with him," Tracker replied. Duke looked over at Will Sullivan and decided to shut up.

Tracker climbed into the ring, and when Duke shouted, "Time!" he and Sullivan moved towards the center and began trading blows.

After a few rounds, Tracker found that he was able to catch many of Sullivan's punches on his elbows and forearms, but the ones that got through rocked him pretty good. The man could punch, there was no doubt about that, but he wasn't very fast. On the other hand, Tracker was hitting him back with some hard shots and they didn't seem to bother him—unless they were to the body.

By the time the session was over, Tracker was convinced of one thing: he was going to have to get a look at Homer Barrow.

"Okay, Will, get cleaned up," he said as they walked away from the center of the ring together.

"You can hit pretty hard, Tracker, you know that?" Sullivan told him.

"Yeah, well, you take them pretty good, too, friend," Tracker replied, adding, "but you take too many."

"That's okay," Will said, waving a hand. "That's always been my style, take two to land one good one." Will Sullivan balled up his fist to show Tracker what "one good one" looked like.

When Sullivan left, Tracker found not only Duke Farrell waiting for him, but with him Deirdre Long.

"Hi," he said to Deirdre.

"Hello. How do you feel?" she asked with concern.

"Sore," he answered, touching his jaw, "and I'll probably have a few more bruises."

She touched his face tenderly and said, "We can take care of that later."

Duke and Tracker exchanged glances, but neither said anything about the obvious change in Deirdre Long's attitude towards the bigger man. They were both thinking the same thing, however, that it could possibly become a problem later on.

Tracker took Deirdre's hand in his but spoke to Duke.

"How did he look on the body shots, Duke?"

Duke shrugged and said, "He looked like he took them okay, why?"

Tracker shook his head and said, "I guess it doesn't show that much, but I can feel him flinch when I hit him. Also, he's not fast enough. He says his style is to take two to land one, but he's taking three and four, at times."

"Barrow's kid is supposed to be good, Tracker," Duke said.

"Well, I want to find out how good he is."

"What do you mean?"

"I want to see him," Tracker said. "If he's that good, I'm not going to let Will fight him. I don't want to see him get killed."

"Wait a minute," Deirdre spoke up. They both looked at her, surprised.

"Well, don't look so surprised," she told them. "I keep my ears open, you know. If Lucas Barrow has been trying to interfere with Will Sullivan's efforts to train

88

for this fight, doesn't that mean he's afraid that Will can win?"

"Not necessarily," Tracker said. "Men like that just like to hedge their bets, even if they know they're likely to win."

"You mean, he'd cheat even if he knew he was going to win?" she asked.

"That's right," Tracker told her.

"I don't understand people like that."

"That makes three of us," Duke said.

"I'm going to get cleaned up. Why don't you two have a talk together?" Tracker suggested.

"Yeah," Duke said, looking at Deirdre. "I'd like that, now that we don't have to be playing roles."

"You mean, we should get to know the real us?" she asked.

"Well, I'd also like to hear some stories about your father," Duke admitted.

"Yeah?" Deirdre asked. "Really?"

"Really."

"Really," Tracker echoed. They both looked at him and he smiled. "Run along, you two. I'll see you later."

Tracker left them standing there and went off to get cleaned up.

He found Will Sullivan drying himself off and asked, "How do you feel, Will?"

"Great, I feel fine."

"How's your head?" Tracker asked, remembering Sullivan's momentary lapse of the day before. It hadn't happened today, but it still concerned him.

"My head's fine, Tracker," Sullivan told him, pulling on a shirt now that he was dry. "It's the kid who's gonna have to worry about head. Believe me."

"Yeah," Tracker said. He picked up a pitcher of water and filled a basin as Sullivan left. Then he looked at the door and added, "I'd like to."

Chapter 19

Tracker was just about finished cleaning up when he heard the door open behind him.

"Duke," he said with his face half buried in a towel, "I thought you and Deirdre were going to—" He stopped short as he turned and saw that it wasn't Duke who had come in, but two men he'd never seen before. They were both armed with knives, but that wasn't what caught Tracker's attention. Although he had never seen either man before, there was something familiar about one of them.

He had a crusted-over gash in the middle of his forehead, which made it more than likely that these were two of the three men he'd fought with in the alley the other night.

"Where's Frank?" he asked, dropping his hands to his side. His gun was hanging on a hook at the other end of the room. He held onto the towel because right now that was the only weapon he had against two men with knives, who he felt sure were there to kill him.

"You don't take advice too good," one of the men—the one without the split forehead—said.

"So now you're here to finish the job, huh?" Tracker asked, edging across the room to where his gun was.

The man without the split seemed to find that funny.

"Go ahead, why don't you, friend?" he asked. "Run for your gun, see if you make it."

Tracker figured that if he ran for his gun he'd have to turn his back on them to draw it, and by that time one or both of their knives would be sticking out of his back. He was going to have to do this without his gun—but then that was the way he solved most of his problems.

He stood his ground, towel dangling from his left hand and said, "I don't need my gun to take care of two flea-bitten pieces of buzzard bait like you two."

The man with the gash on his forehead seemed to take that remark personally.

"I owe you, cowboy," he said, waving his knife with one hand and indicating his forehead with the other. "I'm here to collect."

"Then you come ahead, friend," Tracker said, beckoning him with his empty hand. "Leave your friend behind so he can pick up the pieces when I'm through with you."

Split Forehead started forward, but his partner grabbed his arm and said, "Take it easy. He's trying to rile you. We got to take him together."

Split Forehead pulled his arm away and started for Tracker, while the other man came up behind him.

Tracker flicked the damp towel out and caught Split Forehead in the face, then stepped in and threw a kick. He meant to kick him in the groin, but his foot landed high and banged into the man's belly, forcing the air out of him. Clutching his belly, the man bent over and Tracker put his hands on the other man's shoulders and pushed, forcing him back into his partner.

Both men lost their balance, Split Forehead falling to the floor, but his partner retained his stance and backed away to recover his balance. Tracker took the opportunity to bend over and pick up Split Forehead's dropped knife.

91

"Okay," he said, throwing away the towel, "now things are a little more even, right?"

The standing man looked down at his fallen partner, who was trying to catch his breath, and said, "Come on, Jimmy, get up."

Split Forehead started to get to his feet, but Tracker stepped in and launched a kick that caught him right on the forehead, splitting it open again, and knocking him cold.

"Now it's you and me," he told the other man.

He expected the man to hesitate now that his friend was down and out, but he literally jumped over the fallen body of his partner and caught Tracker by surprise. Neither knife found flesh, but their bodies collided and Tracker staggered back. The other man was not as tall or heavy, but he had the momentum to throw the bigger man off balance.

They clinched and staggered around the room together until Tracker accidentally stepped on the fallen man's ankle. Sensing that Tracker was going to fall, his adversary released his grip. Tracker's grip lightened when he tripped, and as the other pulled away he fell atop the fallen man.

Tracker fell wide open and his opponent lunged down at him with his knife. As he felt the blade slice along his side he angled his own blade up and pushed it through the man's stomach. The other man had been too eager, and he got a belly full of steel for it.

Tracker lay there with the other man's body weighing heavily on him. As he tried to catch his breath he became aware of the fact that his breathing was the only sound in the room.

Both of his attackers were dead.

Chapter 20

Tracker pushed the dead man off him and struggled to his feet. He picked up the towel he had dropped and pressed it to his side, to stop the bleeding. The wound didn't appear to be serious. There was no puncture, just a deep laceration.

Holding the towel tightly against him, he checked the man with the knife in his belly and, as he had expected, found him dead. He was surprised, however, to find that Split Forehead was also dead. His forehead had split open again from the kick and was still leaking blood, but this was not what had killed him. Tracker saw that in falling the man had struck the back of his head on something, and there was more blood and damage there than in front.

He found a chair and sat down, staring at the two dead men. He wished now that one of them was still alive so that he could question them about who had sent them, but he felt sure enough that they had been sent by Lucas Barrow.

He was checking the laceration on his side when the

door opened again, this time admitting Deirdre Long. Her mouth dropped open in surprise as she saw the two dead men, then Tracker with blood on his side and on the towel.

"Tracker!" she cried out, rushing across the room, stepping over the bodies as if they weren't there.

He held his right hand up to her while pressing the left back against his side and said, "I'm fine."

"Let me see," she said, crouching next to him.

"I'm fine," he said again, but he allowed her to look at the wound.

"What happened?" she asked.

"A couple of old friends came to visit," he answered.

She took the towel from him, found a clean side and began to dab at the wound.

"What does that mean?" she asked. She had gotten over her initial shock at finding two dead men at her feet and was now solely concerned with Tracker.

"It means that these are two of the guys who jumped me in the alley the other night," he explained. "I guess they didn't like the idea of me not taking their advice, so they came back to do a better job."

"Yeah, they came back to kill you," she reasoned. "We've got to get this looked at."

"Yeah, okay, but get Duke first," he told her.

"What for?"

"Someone is going to have to talk to the police about this," he said, "and Duke is good at that." He took the towel from her and said, "I'll just sit still and hold this here until you come back with Duke."

"Well, all right," she agreed, looking at him strangely. "I'll be right back. He was in the lobby when I came back here."

"Fine."

She picked her way carefully across the two bodies and left to find Duke. Tracker knew that she must be wondering why he wouldn't want to talk to the police, but he was glad she hadn't asked.

Tracker stood up and walked across the room to his gunbelt. He put the towel aside long enough to strap on the gun, then picked it up again. He folded it, then tucked it inside his shirt. When he stuffed his shirt into his pants, the towel was nestled tightly against the cut,

94

and he felt that would be enough until a doctor could bandage it. He found it odd that he should worry about not being able to spar with Will Sullivan, instead of wondering how he could explain the two bodies to the police so that they wouldn't detain him, or check up on him. One way to do that was to have Duke make the explanations while a doctor was treating him.

When Deirdre returned with Duke, Tracker explained in full what had happened.

"I don't see any problem explaining that to the police," Deirdre commented.

"Well, they might be curious about why I didn't report what happened the other night," Tracker said. He turned to Duke and went on. "Deirdre is going to get a doctor to look at my side. Do you think you can handle the police?"

"Of course," Duke said. "If I can keep them away from you, I will," he promised.

"Thanks." To Deirdre Tracker said, "I'll go up to my room, and you get a doctor to see me up there. Okay?"

"Sure," she said, "whatever you want, but we have to talk about this later, okay?"

He hesitated a moment, then said, "Sure. Tonight we'll talk."

"All right," she agreed. She waited to see if they would leave with her, and when neither one of them moved, she left.

"She's curious," Duke said.

"Yeah, but I don't think she'll be a problem," Tracker replied.

"No, I don't think so, either," Duke said. He looked down at the two men and said, "You figure these are Barrow's men?"

"I can't see it any other way."

"He must really be afraid that Will is going to beat his boy."

"Maybe," Tracker said. "Are you sure you haven't seen anybody we know in town?"

"Not a sign."

"Then it's got to be Barrow." He pressed his hand against his side, pushing the towel tighter against him and said, "I better get upstairs."

"You okay?"

"Fine. It's just a scratch."

"Okay. I'll handle the police and then I'll come up and see how you are."

"Don't make them think I don't want to see them, Duke," Tracker said. "That'll just make them want to see me more."

"I know how to handle it, Tracker," Duke reminded him.

"Yeah, you do," Tracker said, "just don't lay it on too thick, okay?"

"When have you ever known me to lay a con on too thick?" Duke asked. "Leave it to me."

Chapter 21

After the doctor taped the wound and told Tracker not
to do too much running until it healed, Deirdre stayed
behind. They had a few moments before Duke showed
up, so she kissed him tenderly and then pulled her face
away and asked, "What's going on?"

"I thought we were going to talk tonight," he said,
catching her eyes and holding them.

She shrugged and said, "We have some time now,
don't we?"

"I've got work to do," he countered.

"Oh, no, you don't," she told him. "The doctor said
you're supposed to rest."

He shook his head and said, "If I can't spar with Will
for a couple of days—"

"A couple of days?" she asked incredulously.

"The least I can do for him is go out and scout the
competition," he finished.

"It's going to be more than a couple of days before
you can spar again," she said firmly, "and if you try to

go out and scout the competition, some more of Barrow's men will just be able to finish the job."

"Barrow won't have me killed anywhere near him," Tracker said. "He doesn't mind a couple of broken tables at his place, but I'm sure he wouldn't want any bodies lying around—mine or anybody's."

"Why don't you want to talk to the police?" she asked, changing tracks.

"Do you look forward to talking to the police," he asked, "with your checkered past?"

"I was never arrested during my checkered past," she informed him, "and besides, I'm legitimate, now." She narrowed her eyes for a moment, studying him, then said, "You know, we talked last night about my past, and Duke's past, but we didn't talk about your past."

"That's right," he said, "we didn't."

Before she could speak again, there was a knock on the door and Tracker called out, "Come on in."

Duke opened the door and entered the room, looking smugly satisfied with himself.

"How did it go?" Tracker asked. "Any problems?"

"No, everything went fine," Duke said. "As far as the police are concerned, you found the bodies of two men who apparently had a fight and killed each other."

"But they still want to talk to him, don't they?" Deirdre asked.

"Uh, no, they don't," Duke answered.

"Why not?"

"Well, they were just a couple of lowly policemen," Duke told her, and then he turned to Tracker and said, "and you owe me some money."

"You bribed two policemen?" Deirdre asked. "I can't believe this. I'm trying to be legitimate, and I end up tied up with one man who bribes police, and one who's afraid to talk to them."

Duke looked at Tracker, who just shrugged.

"Honey, I have to tell you, Tracker's not afraid of a whole lot of things, and none of them walk on two legs."

"Well, he's certainly afraid to talk about his past," she said.

Tracker stayed quiet and let Duke talk.

"He's not afraid," Duke said. "He might be unwilling, but he's not afraid."

"Two against one," she observed, looking at both of them in turn. "Is this the way it's always going to be?"

"I would prefer to think that the three of us are together," Tracker said. "That we're going to build this place up together."

"Build it up to what?" she asked.

"To just a little more than it is now," Tracker said.

"You know," she said to Tracker, "you don't talk a heck of a lot and when you do talk, you say even less."

"Look, Deirdre. I agreed to help Will Sullivan get ready for a fight, and now I've ended up opposing one of the most powerful men in San Francisco."

"So, quit," she said, but then she put one hand to her mouth and added, "I guess that was foolish."

"It was. I've been beaten up once, and they tried to kill me once. Those kinds of things I don't forget."

There was a darkness in his eyes when he said that, and she felt a chill and had to look away. She believed him, and for the first time since she had met him, he scared her.

"We also have the hotel to worry about," he went on. "We're going to get an offer to buy pretty soon."

"There haven't been any more accidents," Duke spoke up.

"And I hope there won't be," Tracker replied. "But those other incidents didn't happen without reason. They have to be leading up to something."

"I guess so," Duke said.

"Deirdre?" Tracker said.

"Hmm?" she said, looking back at him.

"Are we together on this?" he asked.

"Yeah," she replied, sounding as if she were only half there, "as far as the hotel goes, we're together."

Tracker figured that would have to do, for now.

Chapter 22

Lucas Barrow's dinner was not going down easily. He was choking on the information that had just been given him by Dan Logan.

"Say that again," he told his bodyguard.

Logan fidgeted, then repeated the information.

"Our contact with the police says that Tracker apparently killed Jimmy and Lance."

"Was he taken in?"

Logan hesitated, then shook his head.

"Why the hell not?"

"Somebody decided that it wasn't necessary. Jimmy was killed with his own knife, so they figure Tracker was just defending himself."

"Yeah," Barrow said, "somebody decided—I'll tell you what somebody decided. Somebody decided that making a few extra dollars was more important than arresting Tracker." Barrow removed his napkin from his lap and threw it down on his plate, where it covered his unfinished dinner.

"So what do we do?" Logan asked nervously.

"You do what I told you to do," Barrow replied coldly. "Tracker is dead before the fight, or you are. Hire as many men as you have to, Logan, because you're hiring them to save your life."

Chapter 23

As they walked through the lobby together Deirdre was called to the front desk by Lewis, the little dandy who thought that Farrell and Tracker were "vulgar."

"Can we fire him?" Farrell asked Tracker.

"Does he do his job?"

"Yeah," Duke admitted grudgingly, "and he does it well, too."

"Then forget about firing him just because he doesn't like girls. Let's go to the saloon and get a drink."

On the way through the dining room, Duke said, "Speaking about girls, what are you going to do about Nora?"

"Nora? What about her?"

"She likes you, but now that you're friendly with Deirdre—"

"What about Nora, anyway?" Tracker asked, interrupting him. "I haven't seen her around. The only time I've ever seen her is the two times you sent her to my room."

"Two times?"

"Yeah."

"I only sent her once, my friend," Duke said. "That's what I mean by she likes you."

"Well, where is she?" Tracker asked again as they entered the saloon. "I've never seen her down here."

"Oh, you'd never see her down here, Tracker," Duke assured his friend, and the way he said it told Tracker why.

Tracker waited until they had both ordered beers from Will Sullivan, and when they had them he suggested that they sit at a table.

"Thanks, Will," Duke said to the fighter.

"Sure, Duke."

They sat down opposite each other and Tracker took a pull on his mug of beer before speaking. He leaned across the table and said, "Duke, are you running girls in this hotel?"

"Well..." Duke said, looking sheepish.

"In other words, Nora doesn't work for the hotel—for me—she works for you."

Fiddling with his beer mug, Duke said, "Well, I had to get something going for myself, Tracker. You know, in case you decided that the hotel business wasn't right for us—I mean, you."

"It's us, Duke, don't worry about it," Tracker told him. "I still would like to stay in the background."

"Then you've decided to stick around?"

"I've gone as far as deciding to keep the hotel. What I might do is use it as a base to operate from."

"That makes sense," Duke agreed. "At least you'd always have someplace to come back to."

"I suppose that's one way of looking at it," Tracker conceded.

"And it'll keep me in San Francisco," Duke continued. "This is my kind of town, Tracker."

"Full of marks, huh?"

"There are a lot of nice people here, Tracker," Duke said, defending himself.

"And they have a lot of nice money, right?"

"Tracker..."

"No more girls, Duke."

"Aw, come on..."

"Deirdre is trying to run this hotel legitimately,"

103

Tracker said, "and that's the way we're going to run it."

"Has that girl gotten to you?" Duke asked. Tracker replied with a hard look, and Duke subsided, saying, "All right, never mind. No more girls."

"You can hire Nora and the other girls—"

"Four, altogether."

"—to work here in the saloon. Whatever they can make on the side—on their own—is up to them."

When Duke didn't reply right away Tracker said, "Agreed?"

"Agreed."

"Good. Now that that's settled, let's go onto bigger things. Find me Homer Barrow."

"I don't know if that's such a good idea, Tracker, walking into Barrow's camp."

"Lucas Barrow is not going to pull anything there," Tracker said confidently. "He could have had me killed right in his own place if he wanted to, but he chose to do it here. When I get killed, he's going to want to look as clean as he can."

"I guess you know what you're doing," Duke said.

"Always," Tracker reminded him.

"All right. I'll see what I can find out."

"Well, do it fast. The fight's in four days."

"Right," Duke said. He drained his beer and got up to leave. "I'll get started now." He started to walk away, and then stopped. "Are you going to tell Will what happened out back?"

"Yeah," Tracker answered. "I'll tell him before I leave. He'll have to work hard alone for a couple of days until I can get back in there with him." Then Tracker looked at Duke closely and said, "That is, unless you—"

"Forget it," Duke snapped. "I ain't never been suicidal, and I don't intend to start now."

"No," Tracker replied, watching his friend's retreating back, "I didn't think you would."

Chapter 24

Tracker finished his beer and went to the bar to get another one. When Will put it down in front of him he said, "Let's talk, Will."

"Sure. What's wrong?"

Tracker related to him everything that had happened after he left that morning.

"Jesus, Tracker," Will said, looking concerned, "I'm sorry I got you into this. I guess you want out now, huh?"

"Not on your life," Tracker said, "or mine, Will. I don't appreciate being beaten one night and stabbed another."

"Well, you can't spar anyway, so you might as well pull out," Sullivan reasoned.

"I'll be back in with you in a couple of days, Will," Tracker assured him. "I just got scratched, that's all. You work hard alone for a couple of days, and we'll spar the last two days before the fight. Okay?"

"Sure, it's okay with me. It's you they're trying to kill, not me."

"I guess they figure Barrow's son will do that in the ring," Tracker suggested.

"Then they better change their thinking," Will told him. "I'm gonna take that kid apart."

"Have you ever seen this kid, Will?"

"Yeah, I seen him," Sullivan answered, leaning his powerful forearms on the bar. "He's big."

"Big," Tracker repeated. "Have you ever seen him fight?"

"No, I never have, but that don't worry me, Tracker," Will said. He held up a fist and said, "I'm ready for anybody."

At that point, Sullivan looked towards the front entrance of the saloon and his face froze.

"Oh, shit," he said, softly.

"What's the matter?" Tracker asked.

"I'm ready for anybody," Sullivan said again, and then added, "anybody but her."

Tracker turned and looked at the girl who had just entered the saloon. She was a tall girl, dressed in a man's shirt that failed to hide the thrust of her very large breasts. She was wearing jeans tucked into riding boots, and she stood there with her hands on her hips, glaring at Sullivan. Her hair was a wild mass of red curls that fell to the shoulders, and her full-lipped mouth was set in a tight, thin line.

"Who is she?" Tracker asked.

"Jesus Christ," Sullivan said again, "it's my little sister."

Chapter 25

"Will Sullivan," she shouted, pointing an accusing finger at her brother, "how long did you think you could keep me from finding out?"

Tracker turned to Will and said, "Little sister?"

"Baby sister, really," Will said, "but she's always thought she was my mother."

As the woman approached, Tracker saw what Sullivan had meant by "baby" sister. She was at least twenty years younger than he was, and maybe more.

"Will—" she started as she reached the bar, but her brother interrupted her.

"Please, Shana," he said, "keep your voice down."

"If you will talk to me, Will Sullivan, I'll keep my voice down," she replied angrily.

"Of course I'll talk to you, but not here. Do you want to get me fired, girl?"

The girl compressed her lips and fumed in silence.

"Shana, I want you to meet a friend of mine," Will told his sister.

"One of your drinking buddies, no doubt," the girl accused.

"Shana, this is my friend, Tracker," Sullivan went on, undaunted by his sister's sharp tongue. "Tracker, my baby sister, Shana Sullivan."

"My pleasure, ma'am," Tracker said, removing his hat.

Her flashing green eyes looked at Tracker for the first time, ready to disapprove, but it became apparent that, even against her will, she liked what she saw.

"Well, you don't look like the usual drunken ex-fighters my brother usually has as friends," she remarked, "although your face does look like it's been catching a few fists."

"Your brother's, mostly," Tracker explained. "I've been sparring with him, helping him get ready for his next fight."

Her eyes flashed disapproval once again, and she turned them on her brother.

"You are not fighting again, Will!" she snapped.

"Shana, we can't talk about this here," Sullivan said desperately. He looked at Tracker with pleading eyes.

"Maybe we could have some lunch, Miss Sullivan, and wait until Will is finished behind the bar," Tracker suggested to the girl.

She looked at Tracker again, who was looking back at her expectantly, and then said, "Lunch in the hotel?"

"Yes, of course."

"All right," she said, and then to her brother, "but you're not off the hook, Will Sullivan. I'm not going to stand around while you get yourself killed."

"We'll talk later, Shana," her brother told her. His eyes silently thanked Tracker for getting him "off the hook," at least for a while.

"Let's go into the dining room," Tracker suggested.

"Uh, I'm not dressed—," she started to say, looking embarrassed.

"Don't worry about that," he assured her, taking her by the arm. "I have friends in the hotel."

When they were seated by a disapproving waiter, Tracker ordered for both of them.

"I take it you don't approve of your brother's plans to fight again."

She stared at him and said, "You don't talk like most of my brother's friends."

"Maybe I haven't been hit in the head as much as most of his friends," he suggested. Actually, the reason Tracker spoke better than her brother's friends—and a lot of Westerners—was because he'd had a fairly good education as a young boy, before he had taken to traveling and getting an education of another kind.

"Or him," she added. "If he fights again, he's gonna get killed, Mr. Tracker."

"Just Tracker," he said. "Why does he want to fight again if he knows that?"

"Because he refuses to admit it, and he refuses to admit that he's too old to fight. You been sparring with him, you know he can't beat a younger man."

"Just because a man is younger doesn't make him better," he pointed out. "Experience counts for a lot, Miss Sullivan."

"You can call me Shana," she said, "and that's about all my brother has left, Tracker, his experience. He's almost fifty years old!"

"Fifty?"

"Yeah, I know, he told you he was thirty-eight."

"Forty-three."

"Well, at least he's getting closer. Did you know that he hasn't had a fight in almost two years?"

"No, I didn't."

"Did he tell you that he was knocked out in his last fight?"

"Uh, no, he didn't tell me that, either."

"Did he tell you that the punch that knocked him out wouldn't have knocked me out?" she asked. "No," she went on, "he wouldn't have told you that, either."

"No," Tracker agreed, "he wouldn't have."

"So now that you know, you've got to help me keep him from fighting," she insisted.

Tracker had to admit that she was making a lot of sense, but if Will didn't fight, how would that help him repay Lucas Barrow for the beating and the attempt to kill him?

Then again, even if they called the fight off, they still had four days in which to do that, and he might be able to come up with an idea by then.

109

"Why don't we let him keep training?" he suggested. "We'll figure out something between now and the day of the fight. He seems pretty determined, and arguing with him for four days really won't accomplish anything."

"I can't argue with that," she agreed. "I've been fighting with him for twenty-nine years and it hasn't done me much good."

"All right, then. Let's let him think that I was able to talk you into leaving him alone until after the fight."

She shrugged and said, "Okay," and began to get up.

"You can't leave without having lunch," Tracker said.

Standing, she said, "I still feel a little embarrassed about the way I'm dressed."

"Well, we can take care of that," he said, standing up.

"How?"

"I'll have them send our lunch to my room," he said. "Since we're going to be working together to try and keep your brother from killing himself, we might as well get to know each other a little better, while we're at it."

Chapter 26

Tracker and Shana actually did finish lunch before the natural chemistry between a healthy man and a healthy woman brought them to bed together.

Shana proved how uninhibited she really was only seconds after they had removed each other's clothing. She pushed Tracker onto his back and directed her attention to his long erection. Cradling it between her hands, she began to run her tongue lovingly around the swollen, mushroomlike head of it, then slid it in and out of her mouth. Soon, she was running her tongue along the entire length of the shaft, and the sensations Tracker were feeling were marvelous. The girl knew what she was doing, and for one of the few times in his life, Tracker surrendered himself to a woman and allowed her to be in control.

She continued her oral stimulations for some time, and when she could no longer wait, she raised herself above him and impaled herself on his incredibly hard penis. He felt that he had never been as hard or as long in his life, and when he pierced her lips he couldn't believe how hot and deep she was, or how sensitive his own organ seemed to be.

She began to swivel her hips back and forth, grinding herself against him, tangling her curly red bush with his coarse black one.

He cupped her large, cherry-tipped breasts and began to thumb her nipples. She began to moan aloud and plead with him to keep squeezing them.

He matched the tempo of her hips and continued to squeeze her nipples until the cords on her neck stood out and her entire body shuddered. At that moment, he released himself and allowed his seed to spew into her.

As she slid off him and stretched out beside him she said, "Well, now that we know each other a little better, tell me something."

"What?" he asked without turning his head.

"Why would you agree to help a broken-down old fighter like my brother train for a fight? I mean, what did you think was in it for you?"

"Nothing, really," he answered honestly. "To begin with, I liked him as soon as I met him."

"That's not surprising," she said. "Even the man who knocked him out two years ago liked him."

"Aside from that, it was just something different for me, out of the ordinary."

She regarded him critically for a moment and then said, "I get the feeling that for a man like you, there ain't too many things that are out of the ordinary."

She had that much right, he thought. He'd done a lot of things over the years, but there were still some things he hadn't yet done.

A few, anyway.

Tracker was straight with Shana Sullivan and told her everything that had happened to him since his arrival in San Francisco. He did not tell her that he was half-owner of the hotel they were now in, but he did tell her that he intended to pay Lucas Barrow back, whether Will fought his boy or not.

"I can't say that I blame you for that," she said, touching the bandage on his side. "We didn't open that, did we?" she asked.

112

He looked down at her hand and said, "No...but that doesn't mean that we have to stop trying."

He reached for her and she went into his arms quite willingly, saying, "No, I guess it doesn't."

Chapter 27

Shana told Tracker that she and her brother lived in a section of San Francisco that was primarily Irish, and somewhat less comfortable than Portsmouth Square and its surrounding sections. Tracker told her to go home, and promised to keep in touch.

No sooner had she gone than there was a knock on his door. It was Duke Farrell, and the look on his face told Tracker that all was not well.

"They've got the kid hidden away somewhere," he told his friend.

"Does that mean you can't find him?" Tracker asked.

"No, it just means that it might take a little longer," Duke said. "I've been in town longer than you have, but not long enough to have built up the kind of connections I'd like to have. I'll find him, though, don't worry. There is something else, though, that you might want to worry about."

"What's that?"

"Actually it's not what, it's *who*."

"All right, then, who?"

"Deirdre. You're lucky I saw you come up here with that redhead. Deirdre was on her way up here, but I headed her off and convinced her that they needed her in the kitchen."

"So what would have been the problem?" Tracker asked.

Duke stared at him and said, "Jesus, Tracker. You know how to get women into bed—and I envy you for that—and you know how to handle them once you get them there, but after that you need some lessons."

"From you?" Tracker asked, smiling slightly.

"From me or somebody," Duke said. "You can't be juggling her, Nora and this new redhead of yours."

"The redhead is Will Sullivan's sister, Shana," Tracker explained. "She's here to try and keep Will from fighting."

"Why?"

"Because she says he'll be killed," Tracker said and explained everything that Shana had told him about her brother's boxing career, of late.

"Jesus, and he still wants to fight?"

"What if I told you one more con would kill you, Duke?" Tracker asked.

Duke thought it over a moment, then admitted, "Yeah, I see your point."

"I've convinced her to leave him alone for the next four days," Tracker added.

"You're going to let him fight?"

"I don't know. I think that's going to have to be his decision to make, don't you? I can't keep him from fighting if he wants to, but maybe I can make him consider everything before he makes that decision."

"And what about Barrow?" Duke asked.

"Barrow is mine, Duke," Tracker said, his eyes darkening as they did when he was deadly serious about something. "All mine. I owe him a lot, and I'm going to pay him back."

Duke backed off on the subject of Barrow and said, "What about Deirdre?"

"I like Deirdre," Tracker said. "I like Nora, and I like Shana. I like women, Duke, you know that, but I'm not built to concern myself with the wants and

115

needs of any one of them. Maybe that's a flaw in me, but it's one I'll have to put up with...and so will they."

Duke shook his head and said, "Women are more dangerous than you think, Tracker."

Tracker placed one large hand on his friend's shoulder and said, "Your concern touches me, Duke...but is it for me, or Deirdre? Or maybe Nora?"

"They're good kids, Tracker, both of them. I'd hate to see either one of them get hurt."

"I'm not out to hurt anybody, Duke," Tracker replied, "except Lucas Barrow. These three women are all adults, they should all know that a night in bed doesn't link us for life."

"Women are funny—"

"Maybe I'm not the one who's underestimating them, Duke," Tracker suggested. "Think about that."

Before either one of them could think about anything else, however, there was a pounding at the door, and they could hear Deirdre yelling outside.

"Tracker! Duke!"

Duke moved quickly to the door and opened it. Deirdre stood outside, the high degree of her alarm showing plainly on her face.

There was something else they noticed about her as well. There was a strong odor of something burning, and it clung to her clothes.

"What's the matter?" Tracker asked as Duke took hold of her arms to steady her.

"Another accident," she told him. "And this one's bad." She paused to catch her breath and then told them, "The kitchen is on fire!"

Chapter 28

The kitchen was indeed on fire, but it was not as bad as they had first thought. When they had first followed Deirdre down to the kitchen it had appeared that the entire room was in flames. As it turned out, only the rear wall had been, and the promptness of the San Francisco Fire Department—one of the first nonvolunteer departments in the country—had saved it.

Until the arrival of the fire department, Tracker, Duke and even Deirdre had worked with some of the employees and some of their neighbors in keeping the back wall doused with as much water as possible.

After the fire was out Duke went in to supervise the kitchen crew as they got everything back in order, and Tracker went with Deirdre to her room so she could bathe and change.

"Do you want to join me?" she asked at her door.

Ordinarily, Tracker would have said yes, but only an hour before he had been with Shana Sullivan, and he didn't know if he was ready for a long session with Deirdre.

"I'd better go downstairs and help Duke," he told her. "I want to see if we can find out where the fire started."

She looked disappointed but did not comment on it. Instead she said, "All right. After I've cleaned up I'll come back down. I want to know where that fire started, too, and whether or not it was an accident."

"Hopefully, by the time you come down, we'll know," he said.

Tracker went back down to the kitchen and discovered that Duke had already found out whether or not it was an accident.

"It couldn't have been," he told Tracker.

"Why not?"

"It didn't start inside," Duke explained. "According to the fire chief, the fire was started outside. How could that happen accidentally?"

"Somebody had to have set that wall on fire from the outside," Tracker agreed.

"So, another accident that's no accident," Duke said. "Who the hell is behind it?"

"I have a feeling we'll be finding that out very shortly," Tracker said. "Why don't we get cleaned up? I think they can handle things down here."

"What about Deirdre?"

"She's getting cleaned up now. Leave her a message that we're doing the same. We can meet her in the dining room. I think I'd like to make some plans for the time when we finally get the offer to buy."

"I wish I could be as sure as you that that's what all of this is leading up to."

"Come up with an alternative, and I'll be glad to listen," Tracker said.

"If I think of one, you'll be the first to know," Duke promised him.

Duke left the message for Deirdre with one of the kitchen crew, and then he and Tracker went to their respective rooms to clean up. They agreed to meet in the dining room in half an hour.

Tracker would have preferred to soak in the tub for a long period of time, but instead he simply removed his shirt and washed his face and upper body thoroughly. He could soak the charred wood smell from his entire body later on, but now he wanted to get downstairs and meet with Duke and Deirdre.

He thought about what Duke had told him about taking a chance by juggling three women. None of the three were very important to him right now as a person, but Deirdre was the one he felt he would be around the longest, since she owned a share of the hotel. She was the one whose good graces he would want—not need—since they were essentially in business together.

He decided that if he were to meet Shana Sullivan again it would be away from the hotel. Nora he decided not to meet again. If she showed up in his room, that would be a different story, but he would neither invite nor bring her there himself.

He dressed in some of the less formal clothes that Duke had supplied him with, and made a mental note to ask Duke to have someone do his laundry for him.

Dressed and feeling somewhat refreshed, even though he already had had a couple of workouts that day—one with Shana, and one with the fire, he went downstairs to the dining room to find Deirdre and Duke already there waiting for him, their heads together in conversation.

He wondered for a moment what kind of feelings Duke might have for her. He had called her a "good kid," but what did he really feel.

As he approached the table they both looked up and he heard Deirdre say, "Here he is."

"Hope I didn't keep you waiting," Tracker said as he sat down.

"Duke has told me that the fire was no accident," Deirdre said. "What do we do about this?"

"I think we'll get an offer pretty soon," Tracker told both of them. "Here's what I'd like you both to do. I don't want any buyer to meet just one of you. When he comes in here and asks for the owner, I want you both to meet with him. Deirdre, don't talk to anybody without Duke, all right?"

Deirdre seemed to take this personally. She was sure that Tracker wouldn't mind her being there when Duke was talking to someone with her. He just didn't trust her to be able to handle it by herself.

"Wait a minute, Tracker," she said firmly. "You're

119

forgetting who my father was. Because I'm a woman you don't think I'm able to handle situations that Duke could?"

Tracker started to reply, then stopped himself. He threw a look at Duke, rephrased what he had been going to say so that she couldn't possibly take any further offense.

"Deirdre, I know all about what kind of a man your father was," he said.

"He was the best," she said, "and Duke knows it."

She looked to Duke for support, and he applied some by saying, "That's for sure."

"Okay, I don't deny that," Tracker assured her. "And I mentioned it myself because I want you to understand that I realize that your father taught you everything you know." In trying to appease her, he found that he was also convincing himself, so when he said to her, "I'm sure you can handle anyone you put your mind to handling," he actually believed it himself.

Deirdre seemed to sense that she wasn't just being humored, but she didn't want to give in to Tracker too easily.

"I'll agree that if Duke is easy to find when the situation arises, I won't say anything until we're together."

Tracker exchanged glances with Duke and then said, "All right, agreed."

"You don't want to be there yourself?" Duke asked.

"I'll be there," Tracker said, "but you'll be the only ones who know I am. We'll set that up, too. I want to be able to see who's doing the talking, without him seeing me."

"Or her," Duke offered. "Without her seeing you."

Tracker looked surprised, but in a satisfied tone of voice Deirdre chimed in and said, "Yeah," with a big smile.

Chapter 29

That evening Tracker went to the saloon to talk to Will Sullivan. When he saw Nora there he was surprised, until he remembered that he had told Duke to hire her. She looked lovely, with her hair swept atop her head, wearing a low-cut, blue gown, but he stood by his original decision not to invite her to his room.

"Hi, Tracker," she said, obviously happy to see him.

"Hello, Nora," he replied. "I didn't know you worked down here."

She nodded and said, "Started today. It's convenient, isn't it?" she asked.

He knew what she meant but pretended not to.

"I suppose. I have to talk to the bartender. See you, uh, sometime."

He had almost said, "See you later," which she probably would have interpreted as an invitation. As he walked past her she gave him an odd look, wondering what it was she could have done to change his attitude towards her.

"Will," he greeted, leaning on the bar.

"Where did you and Shana disappear to this afternoon," Will said, planting a beer in front of him, "or shouldn't I ask?"

"Don't ask," Tracker said. "She'll be off your back for the next four days."

"Thank the Lord," Will said, "and you. How did you manage that? That girl is stubborn as all get-out."

"I convinced her," was all Tracker would say. "She's off your back, but now I'll be on it."

Sullivan frowned and said, "What's that supposed to mean?"

"We have to talk."

"What did she tell you?" the fighter demanded.

"A few things."

He pounded the bar top and asked, "Did she tell you I was fifty years old? That's a damned lie—"

"That was the least of what she told me," Tracker said, cutting him off, "and she only told me that you were almost fifty."

"Well, it's all lies," Will insisted, licking his lips. "Does this mean you're not going to help me anymore?"

"It means that we have to talk, Will," Tracker assured him. "That's all it means...for now. I'll wait until you get off."

"All right," Will said in a resigned tone.

Tracker took his beer and moved to a corner table. The place was fairly busy, and it took a few moments for Nora to circulate through the room and get back to him.

"Mind if I sit down?" she asked.

"That's your job, isn't it?" he asked.

She slid a chair out and sat down.

"What's wrong, Tracker?"

"What could be wrong?"

"Did I say, or do, something wrong?"

"You were fine, Nora."

"Then can I come to your room tonight?"

"Wouldn't you rather find someone who will pay you for your time?" he asked her.

"No," she answered simply.

"I'm sorry, Nora, not tonight. I'm going to be busy."

"Tomorrow?"

"I don't know."

"Is there...another woman?" she asked him.

He put his beer down and leaned forward.

"There have been a lot of women, Nora, and there will be a lot more," he explained, making it as simple as he thought he could.

She stared at him for a moment, then whispered, "I see, and I was just one of them?"

"I'm sorry, Nora," he replied, "but that's the way it is—that's the way I am."

She laughed without any trace of humor and said, "I guess it is pretty funny, isn't it? A whore, falling in love? After all, I am just a whore, right?"

"Nora—" he said, touching her hand, but she pulled it away as if he had scalded her with his touch.

"That's all right," she said quickly, making fists out of her hands and holding them shoulder high. "Don't apologize. I should apologize." She stood up, hesitated, then said, "I'm sorry," and turned to quickly walk out of the saloon. Tracker stared after her for a few moments, wondering if he should go after her, but then decided not to. What would be the point? What the hell business did she have falling in love with him, anyway? Did she really expect him to feel the same way after going to bed with her twice?

Tracker let his mind wander back, but he could not recall ever having been in love. He wasn't even sure he would know what the emotion felt like.

He finished his beer and signaled Will for another one, then settled down and waited for the old boxer's shift to end, so they could talk about his fighting career.

Such as it was.

Chapter 30

In the short time that he had been in San Francisco, and at the hotel, Tracker had decided that the saloon was his favorite place at Farrell House—a name he was still thinking about changing. When Will's shift behind the bar was over, they remained in the saloon to have their talk.

Will came to his table with another beer and sat down.

"Okay, let's talk," he said to Tracker.

Tracker related to Will Sullivan everything his sister Shana had told him, and then asked him to explain all or part of it away.

"Can't explain it away," Sullivan admitted. "I did get knocked out in my last fight, and the punch that knocked me out wouldn't have bothered me in the old days." He hesitated, formulating his thoughts, then went on. "Uh, yeah, getting knocked out like that scared me and I didn't fight for two years, but it's different now."

"Why?"

"This kid, Barrow, he's supposed to be pretty good.

124

If I take him out, I could get a shot at the championship. Even if I lose that fight, at least I had a shot at the title, you know? That's why I got to fight Barrow and beat him. Ain't nothing gonna keep me from beating him, not even his old man and all of his money."

"Well, you'll get the fight, Will, that's for sure. Lucas Barrow just wants to hinder your chances of being in peak condition when you step in with his son. In his mind, he might be afraid that you'll get lucky."

"Luck ain't gonna have anything to do with it," Sullivan said fervently. "He's gonna run into one of these," Will added, raising a fist, "and it's gonna be all over."

Tracker remembered what had happened to Will the first day of sparring, when he had run into Tracker's last right of the session. Tracker hadn't mentioned it before, but he did now.

"You hit hard, Tracker," Sullivan told him, by way of an explanation.

"But I'm not a pro, Will. This kid, Barrow—"

"It was my first sparring session," Will said, interrupting him. "My timing was off, you caught me just right. It didn't happen again, did it?"

Tracker didn't point out the fact that they only sparred one more time after that.

"Okay, Will, okay," he said, calming the other man down. "All I want you to do is think about it, okay? Is a shot at the champ worth your life? That's what I want you to ask yourself, and decide."

"You ain't gonna stop me from fighting?"

Tracker sat back and said, "How the hell could I do that, Will? The only one who can stop you is you. I just hope you make the right decision."

"I got to make the decision that's right for me," Sullivan pointed out.

"That's all I'm asking you to do, Will," Tracker said, standing up. "While you're at it, work on that belly, huh?"

"Sure," Will answered, touching his mid-section. "Sure."

Tracker picked up his mug, finished his beer and

started to leave when Will asked, "What are you gonna be doing?"

"Me?" Tracker replied. "I still have to scout the competition. I'm going to try and find young Homer Barrow and see if we really have anything to worry about."

Chapter 31

After breakfast the following morning, Tracker asked Duke how he was coming with finding the younger Barrow.

"I'm hoping to get something on him today," Duke said.

"We've only got a few days left," Tracker reminded him.

"I know." As Tracker started away Duke said, "Here's something that might interest you."

"What?"

"Nora quit that job you had me give her."

"When?"

"She decided last night, and told me this morning. You wouldn't know anything about that, would you?" Duke asked.

"We had a talk last night," Tracker admitted.

"What did you tell her?"

"The same thing I told you, Duke," he answered testily. "I'm sorry if what I told her was the cause of her quitting, but there's nothing I can do about that."

"No, I guess there isn't," Duke agreed.

"Let's drop it, okay?" Tracker suggested. "I won't tell you who to con, and you don't tell me who to take to bed—or how many times. Deal?"

"Sure, it's a deal," Duke agreed. "Are you, uh, going to tell Deirdre the same thing you told Nora?"

"Duke," Tracker said warningly.

"I just don't want to see the kid get hurt," Duke explained.

"Well, I don't have any intentions of hurting her, not if we're going to go on being partners. Satisfied?"

"I suppose I'll have to be," Duke replied.

"Can we drop all that now?" Tracker asked.

"All right, we'll drop it."

"Good. There's a question I want to ask that I should have asked you before."

"What?"

"Who is promoting this fight between Will and Barrow's kid?"

"Guy named Luke Short. He's a gambler, and I understand he's also pretty good with a gun, judging from what I heard about Leadville—"

"I know all about what happened in Colorado, Duke," Tracker said, interrupting him.

"Do you know Short, Tracker?"

"Yeah, Luke and I have crossed paths before."

"Friend or foe?" Duke asked with interest.

Tracker touched a finger to his right cheekbone and said, "I don't think either one of us was quite sure about that at the time."

Duke looked surprised and said, "You were in Leadville?"

"I've been in a lot of places, Duke," Tracker reminded him, "and I've met a lot of people."

"Is this going to complicate things?" Duke asked.

Tracker thought for a moment and then said, "No, I don't think so. As a matter of fact, it might help. I'll see you later, all right?"

"Where are you going?"

"I'm going to find Luke Short and have a talk with him."

"Wouldn't it be easier if you knew what hotel he was staying in?"

Tracker stopped, turned and looked at his grinning friend.

"Are you going to make me ask then?"

Duke kept grinning for a few moments, then said, "He's staying at the Bella Union, in Portsmouth Square."

"Well, Luke always did like to go first class," Tracker remembered.

"That's Portsmouth Square, all right," Duke agreed. "First class—except for Lucas Barrow."

Chapter 32

Tracker went to the Bella Union, a somewhat less ostentatious version of the Alhambra, although it had a little less room for gambling, and a little more room for guests. It was more hotel than gambling house or saloon.

Walking through Portsmouth Square, Tracker started to feel an itch for the wide-open spaces again. This particular part of the city was much too inhabited for his taste. Maybe the time was coming for him to leave San Francisco. He had learned at an early age that the wanderlust ran deep in his blood, and he hoped he could keep it from kicking up for at least three or four more days. Fighting that feeling would make it extra hard for him to concentrate on what he felt he had to do.

Tracker asked for Short's room number at the desk, and a somewhat harried, spinsterish desk clerk blurted it right out to him without a second thought. For a man of Luke Short's stature, that kind of thing could prove fatal. Tracker decided to approach Short in that spirit, letting him know that the desk was not above giving his room number out to just anybody.

He went up to Short's room and knocked on the door. When the door opened, Short stood there, looking no different than he had in Leadville almost two years ago, when they had first met. He was a dapper, medium-sized man in his late thirties or early forties, with a bushy mustache and dark, piercing eyes which made clear the fact that the man was utterly devoid of fear. Part of the reason for his fearlessness was his proficiency with the .45 even now he was wearing on his hip.

Actually the incidents in Leadville were not all they had been blown up to be. Shortly after Short had arrived in Leadville, he had occasion to draw his weapon. But he only used it the first couple of times as a club, to get his point across. Finally, however, someone had decided to really test him, and Tracker had been standing at the very same faro table at the time. Another gambler decided to fiddle with Short's chips, and after an exchange of words, both men drew their guns. Short was the faster of the two. The other man did not die, and no charges were brought against Short, but just the same he chose to leave town soon after. On that occasion he had been toting a special sawed-off Colt revolver in a leather-lined pocket of his trousers.

"Where's that little sawed-off Colt?" Tracker asked him.

Short frowned a moment, as if trying to place Tracker, but no one could forget a man of his size and proportion.

"Tracker, isn't it?" Short asked.

"It is. Can I come in?"

"How'd you know where I was?" Short asked.

"I just up and asked the desk clerk and she gave me your room number. That could turn out to be pretty unhealthy for a man like you, couldn't it?"

"Damn it!" Short snapped. "Yes, it could. I'll have to speak to the management about it." At that point he stepped back and said, "Sure, come ahead in."

Tracker stepped past him and Short closed the door behind him after first checking the hall.

"A drink?" he asked, indicating a bottle of whiskey on a table by the bed.

"Don't mind if I do."

"Is this a social visit?" Short asked. "How'd you know I was in San Francisco?"

He handed Tracker a drink and remained standing while Tracker sat in a chair.

"Well, no, it's not a social visit," Tracker replied, "and I knew you were in town because we're involved in the same thing, you and I."

"We are?" Short asked, looking surprised. "I had no idea you were anywhere near San Francisco. What is it that we're both involved in?"

"The fight between Will Sullivan and Homer Barrow."

"Homer—," Short started, and then stopped. "Oh, you mean the Kid Barrow fight? Who's Sullivan, the other guy?"

"The Kid Barrow fight?" Tracker asked, finding that very interesting. "Is that what it's being called?"

"Well, what would you call it?" Short asked. "The other guy is just an opponent, right?"

"Is that how you feel?" Tracker demanded.

"Hey, whoa," Short warned, "ease off, Tracker. Suppose you tell me what your connection is, and why you're here."

Tracker warned himself to go lightly with Short. He wasn't here to alienate the man.

"My connection is with the 'opponent,' as you call him, Will Sullivan. I've been helping him get ready for the fight, and I presented myself to Lucas Barrow as his manager."

Short digested the information, then said, "I'll admit I'm surprised. I didn't know you had any connection with boxing."

"Well, I didn't until a few days ago. Sullivan needed a sparring mate. It seems that before I came along, he wasn't able to find anyone willing to buck Lucas Barrow by helping him."

Short frowned and said, "Wait a minute. You think Barrow was keeping Sullivan from getting a sparring partner?"

"And from getting a place to train," Tracker added.

"What makes you think Barrow was behind it?" Short asked, showing what appeared to be genuine interest.

Tracker decided to tell Short what had happened to him ever since he had met Will Sullivan.

"I can't argue with the fact that you had a fight with his bodyguard," Short said after the explanation. "But what makes you think that the two incidents with these other two men are connected with him?"

"As soon as I talked to the man, Luke," Tracker said, "I knew he was behind it, but maybe you need time to think over everything I've just told you."

"Maybe I do," Short admitted. "I want this fight to be on the up-and-up, Tracker. It can only hurt my reputation if both fighters aren't at their peaks and don't put on a good show for the paying customers."

"I'm at the Farrell House hotel," Tracker told him.

"That's not in the Square, is it?" Short asked.

"No, a couple of blocks outside. My tastes aren't as expensive as yours."

"You look a little better dressed than you did in Leadville," Short pointed out.

"I've had a run of good luck with poker," Tracker admitted.

"Are you gambling more these days?" Short asked. "Cards, boxing, I don't recall you being that involved with games of chance. Seems to me you used to hunt for a living—"

"My business has changed since then," Tracker said quickly, not wishing to discuss his own past, "but not to gambling. This is just a diversion for me." He got up and tossed off his drink.

"Well, not for me," Short said. "If Barrow is tampering with your fighter, I want to know about it. I'll look into it and let you know what I find out."

"All right, but I'll be looking into a few things myself, as well. Do you know where 'Kid Barrow' is training?"

"No, I don't. Why?"

"I'd just like to get a look at him, check out the competition," Tracker explained.

"Well, I haven't seen your fighter, Tracker, but I have seen Barrow. He's a big, healthy kid. With a little seasoning, he could probably go right to the top."

"If his father has anything to say about it," Tracker said, "it might be even sooner than you think."

133

"You think his old man wants to buy him the title?" Luke Short asked.

"You've dealt with men like Lucas Barrow before," Tracker reminded him. "What do you think?"

Tracker didn't wait for Short to answer. He left him to do just that, think about it.

Chapter 33

Tracker, instead of entering the hotel through the front door, went in through the saloon. Will Sullivan was behind the bar and waved him over when he came in.

"What's the matter?" Tracker asked.

"That dandy little clerk was in here looking for you a couple of minutes ago."

"What did he want?"

"He was all excited about something. He said that Miss Long was looking for you."

"Where'd he go?"

"Back behind his desk, I guess. What's it all about, Tracker? Are you more than just a guest—"

"I'll talk to you later, Will," Tracker said and hurried out through the dining room. He had a feeling he knew why Lewis was looking for him.

The buyer must have finally shown up.

"Lewis," he called as he approached the front desk.

The little dandy looked up and saw the massive figure of Tracker bearing down on him. He had succeeded in avoiding the big man so far, but that was not to be any longer. He had been glad when he couldn't find him for Miss Long, but now he was here and there was nowhere to go.

"Mister...uh...Tracker."

"I understand you were looking for me?"

"Uh, yes, sir, I was. That is, Miss Long was."

"What did she want?"

"I can't really say, sir, I—"

"Well, where is she now?" Tracker demanded. The rising volume of his voice caused Lewis to flinch.

"Uh, she and Mr. Farrell went up to the second floor with a man who was asking for the owner of the hotel."

Tracker slammed his hand down on the desk, making Lewis jump.

"Thanks, Lewis," he said.

He started up the stairs two at a time. The buyer had made his move, and that meant that Deirdre and Duke had taken him up to the room they had agreed to set aside for this meeting. There was an adjoining room through which Tracker planned on eavesdropping without being seen, and that was where he was headed now.

He used the key given him by Deirdre to get into the room, and then moved to the connecting door. He could hear some conversation going on next door, but he couldn't make out what was being said. He'd have to take a chance on opening the door a crack, just enough to make out what was being said, and maybe to get a quick look at the man who was talking to Duke and Deirdre.

He turned the knob slowly and began easing the door open, grateful that it was apparently kept in good condition and didn't creak.

"...really don't have any intentions of selling the hotel," he heard Duke Farrell saying. He couldn't see anyone yet, but he could hear clearly now.

"Not even at double my original offer?" a man's voice asked.

"I'm afraid not."

"That sounds strange," the man said. "This place cannot be making so much money that you would turn down such an offer."

136

"Well, if that's the case," Tracker heard Deirdre speak up, "why do you want it?"

"Well, my people feel that they can build this place up into a money-maker," the man answered.

"That's funny," Duke said. "That's also the way we feel. Tell me, who are 'your people'?"

"I'm afraid I can't divulge the name of my principal, but he and his associates are very interested in buying this building."

"Interested enough to cause some accidents to force us out?" Deirdre asked impulsively, and Tracker flinched, and thought he could even feel Duke flinch.

"Accidents?" the man's voice asked. "Oh, yes, I seem to recall hearing that you were having some problems. There was a fire just yesterday, wasn't there?"

"There was," Duke said quickly, sounding as if he were trying to speak before Deirdre could, "but there was very little damage."

"Well, that's very good to hear," the man said. Tracker opened the door a little more in an effort to get a look at the speaker, but the best he could do was to get a look at half of Duke's face.

"I believe I shall leave you alone to talk about my offer, Miss Long, Mr. Farrell," the man said. Apparently, he was getting ready to leave, and Tracker felt he would finally get a look at his face.

"I don't think we'll change our minds, Mr. Clark," Duke said.

"Talk it over anyway," the man called Clark said. Tracker heard footsteps and fastened his eyes on the front door of the room. Unfortunately, the man walked to the door and left without turning around again. It was too late to run out into the hall to get a look at him, and there was really no need to. Deirdre and Duke had seen him, and from the way their conversation had ended, he would be back.

Tracker opened the connecting door wide and walked into the other room.

"You heard?" Deirdre said.

"Yeah. I came into the hotel just a few minutes after you were looking for me. I figured this was why you wanted me."

"How much did you hear?" Duke asked.

137

"Double the price, and I heard Deirdre ask about the accidents," he said. Duke rolled his eyes and Deirdre rushed to her own defense.

"Okay, maybe I shouldn't have asked that right out like that, but he was so calm he bothered me."

"It's all right," Tracker assured her, "but next time let Duke do the talking, okay?"

"No," she snapped, "it's not okay. I thought we went through that already. I can handle anybody, remember?"

Tracker held up his hands and backed off, saying, "You're right. I'm sorry."

His ready apology caught her off guard, but she replied, "All right."

Tracker turned to Duke and said, "Did you know him at all?"

"Never saw him before," Duke answered. "But I'll tell you one thing. He's a smooth one."

"Is he working a con?"

"I don't think so."

So that Deirdre wouldn't feel she was being left out Tracker said to her, "What about you?"

"No, I feel the same way. I think he's just fronting for somebody, like he said—his 'principal.'"

"Yeah, I agree," Duke said.

"He'll be back, then," Tracker said, "once he thinks he's given you two enough time to think over his offer."

"I don't have to think it over, Tracker," Deirdre said. "And there's something I want to talk to you about," she added.

"Oh, what?"

"How long do I have to keep on calling you Tracker?" she asked, folding her arms and looking at both of them.

"Don't look at me," Duke told her. "I don't know his first name, either."

She wasn't sure Duke was telling the truth, but she turned her full attention on Tracker and waited for an answer from him.

"As long as I have to keep calling you Deirdre," he answered.

"Now what does that mean?" she asked him, looking puzzled. "That's my name."

He smiled at her and said, "That's what I mean."

138

Chapter 34

Deirdre went off to do whatever it was she did for the hotel, and Tracker and Duke went to Tracker's room.

"Did you talk to Short?"

"I did. He doesn't like the idea that Barrow might be tampering with Will's training, but he's also not quite ready to accept it as a fact."

"So?"

"So, he's going to look into it."

"And what are we going to do?"

"We're going to look into it, too. What have you got on the kid's location?"

"We've got it narrowed down, and we should have something before the day is out—maybe by tonight."

"Good. What about this guy Clark?" Tracker asked. "What did he say his first name was?"

"Richard."

"And you've never seen him before?"

"Never seen or heard of him."

"What'd he look like? I wasn't able to get a look at him."

"He was tall, dark hair, maybe forty years old. He wasn't carrying a gun."

"No shoulder rig?"

Duke shook his head and said, "Nothing, I'm sure of it."

"He must be pretty sure of himself, then," Tracker reasoned.

"That's for sure. When do you think he'll be back?"

"Tomorrow, probably."

"What do you think they want this place for?"

"Probably just what he said they wanted it for, to make money. The people he represents probably already own a couple of places in the Square."

Duke looked as if he were suddenly struck with an idea.

"You think he could be acting for Lucas Barrow?"

That struck Tracker as a good possibility.

"Or somebody like him."

"How many could there be like him?" Duke asked.

"Not many, I hope. Why don't you go out and see if you can't scout up that kid. I'd like to get a look at him today."

"Okay, Tracker," Duke said, heading for the door. "By the way, are you going to tell her your first name?"

"No, and neither are you," Tracker told his friend.

"Okay, okay, take it easy."

Duke had found out Tracker's first name by accident years ago, and had never revealed it to anyone. Tracker always wondered what his parents must have been thinking when they named him.

"Get going, Duke. I want to get all of this settled so I can get moving."

"You going to leave?"

"For a while. I'm getting kind of crowded, you know?"

"Actually, I kind of like it here, Tracker."

"That's good. You can keep running the place until I get back, but let's get both this fight business and the accidents settled."

"Right, I'll see you later."

Duke left and Tracker sat down. He'd just about made up his mind about what he was going to do with the hotel. He'd work from it and, as Duke had said, he'd have someplace to come back to when his job was over.

140

Tracker had done a lot of things in his life. He'd even been a lawman once, and a bounty hunter for a long time. He'd tired of that, however, when he was forced to bring back more men dead than alive. Since Leadville, he'd been working as a sort of a salvage expert. When someone lost something of value, they could hire Tracker to get it back for them, one way or another. His fee was half the value of whatever it was he was salvaging. He'd run afoul of the law on occasion, which was why he didn't have any desire to talk to the police here in San Francisco. He felt that if they became aware of his presence in town he'd have no peace, but the way Duke had handled them gave him an idea.

If he paid them off well enough, he'd be able to operate from the hotel without being bothered by the police. The hotel would be someplace where he could relax between jobs, and he could take a job only when he felt San Francisco closing in on him. The hotel would guarantee that he would have enough money so that he could turn down any job he didn't want.

If he was going to put this plan into effect, however, there was one thing he was going to have to do, and that was take care of Lucas Barrow. He had killed two of Barrow's men, and he was helping Will get in shape to outbox his son. Barrow wouldn't forget that, expecially if Will should beat his son. He'd never let Tracker exist in peace, so Tracker was going to have to take care of him now, and he could use the fight to do it.

If he lived long enough. Barrow had already tried to have him killed once, so he could be expected to try again. Tracker wished he knew just how many men Barrow had. He could use somebody like Luke Short on his side, and if Short became convinced that Barrow was trying to tamper with his fight plans—and his reputation as well—then he thought Short would fight on his side.

That was the first order of business, then—to convince Short that Barrow was indeed trying to "buy" the fight for his boy.

Chapter 35

"Tracker did what?" Lucas Barrow demanded.

"He went to the Bella Union, to see Luke Short," Dan Logan said again.

Barrow rubbed his jaw and considered the implications of that. Tracker may have gone to Short to tell him that Barrow was tampering with Will Sullivan. He couldn't prove it, but it might start Short thinking. Short was promoting the fight. If something went wrong with it, it would damage his reputation. Short might even decide to come after Barrow himself.

"Danny boy," he said to Logan, "we may just find out how fast you really are with that gun."

"I can take Tracker," Logan said.

"With a gun, maybe," Barrow said, "but Tracker is not a gunman, at least, not that I've heard. I've had him checked out. He was a bounty hunter for a long time, brought more men back dead than alive, and only a few of them were shot. He's a big man, Danny, and it got so he liked to kill men with his hands."

"He didn't kill me," Logan said, as if bragging.

"No, he didn't," Barrow agreed. "Seems like our friend Mr. Tracker got tired of it, and changed his line of work."

"To what?"

"That I'm not sure of, but I don't intend to leave him alive long enough to find out."

"I'll kill him, don't worry," Logan said.

"And you may have to do it yourself this time," Barrow told him, "but take some of the boys with you, just to back you up."

"I'll take care of him."

"What about Short, Logan?"

"What?"

"Can you take Luke Short with a gun?"

Logan smiled. Barrow had not let him use his gun very often since he'd hired on as the rich man's bodyguard, but now he was talking Tracker and Luke Short. If he killed Short, it would enhance his reputation.

"I can take anybody, Mr. Barrow," Logan said, fondling his gun. "Anybody at all."

"Well, we may get the chance to find out if you're right," Barrow told him. "This is Wednesday. You've got until Saturday to kill Tracker, one way or another."

"What about Short?"

"That's up to him," Barrow said. "If Tracker told him something about me, Short might decide to come after me. If he does, he's all yours, and you'll get a bonus."

A bonus, plus a hell of a reputation.

"Look at you," Barrow said. "You young pup, you can't wait to draw on Short, can you? Well, even if you kill him, you'll have your hands full. Short's got friends, big friends. Wyatt Earp, Bat Masterson, Doc Holliday. Can you take them, Danny boy?"

Logan touched his gun and felt a thrill. He had always thought he was faster than anybody with a gun, and now he might finally get to prove it. Twenty-four, he was, and already they were lined up in his sights. Short and Holliday were more gamblers than gunmen, but they had reps as both. He could take them. Wyatt Earp had a rep with a gun, but Logan felt pretty sure he could take him, too. Bat Masterson was the only one who he really thought was anywhere near as fast as

143

him, but he'd try and arrange it so that Masterson was last, with the deaths of his friends preying on his mind.

Logan wasn't only faster than all of them, he was smarter, too.

"Don't worry, Mr. Barrow," he said, touching his gun again. "When it comes to a gun, I can take anybody."

Barrow hoped the kid wasn't just fooling himself. He hoped the kid wouldn't get himself killed.

At least, not until he killed Tracker.

Chapter 36

When Tracker and Duke alighted from the horse-and-buggy cab, they found themselves in a section of the city that was about as different from Portsmouth Square as you could get.

"Are you sure about this?" Tracker asked. "I can't see Lucas Barrow choosing this part of town for his kid to train in."

"If he wanted to keep him under wraps, could you think of a better part of town?" Duke asked frankly.

Tracker was forced to agree. It was the last place but one would associate Lucas Barrow with.

"Which building?" he asked.

"I've got an address," Duke replied.

As they walked along the street, looking for the correct building number, Tracker said, "This was awful sudden, wasn't it?"

"What, finding the kid?"

Tracker nodded and said, "Yeah, complete with address and everything."

Duke stopped walking and asked, "You think we're being lead by the nose?"

"It's a possibility," Tracker admitted. "Did you bring a gun?"

"Uh, yeah, I've got one," Duke said, touching the weapon that was tucked into his belt. Tracker wore his .45 on his hip, as always.

"Let's go," he told Duke. Reluctantly Duke started walking along again. Reluctantly, because it was beginning to look as if things might get physical. Fights and gunplay, those two things fit Tracker more than they did him. No, that was wrong. They actually didn't fit him at all. He was used to talking himself out of tight spots, not shooting his way out, or slugging his way out.

Tracker was right. His contacts coming up with an exact address was a little sudden.

"Um, are you sure you don't want to think twice about this?" Duke asked.

"There's the building," Tracker said, pointing. He hadn't even heard Duke's question, he was so intent on finding the building.

"Yeah, that's it, all right. What do we do, knock on the door and ask if we can come in and watch the competition work out?" Duke asked sarcastically.

"Let's see if there's a back door," Tracker suggested. Duke wasn't sure Tracker was even aware of him. He followed his friend down the block, through an alley, and around to the back of the building in question.

"This is it," Tracker said, only half aloud. He tried the back door and tried it. "Locked," he muttered. Duke folded his arms across his chest and leaned against the building, watching the big man examine the building for a way in.

"Window," Tracker was saying, running his eyes over the building, "another window...too high...there's a window—"

He moved away from Duke to a window that was too high for the smaller man to reach, but not for Tracker. He stretched up, grasped the sill and pulled himself up so he could peer in the window.

"There they are," he said, and Duke pushed away

146

from the wall and walked to where his friend was dangling.

"Get under me," Tracker told him, "I want to see if this window will open."

"How do you expect to get in without being seen?"

Tracker peered through the window again. He could see two people in the next room, moving around inside a ring. He only saw them fleetingly as they moved in and out of sight. The room was totally dark.

"They're in the next room," Tracker whispered. "If I can get this window open I can get in with nobody noticing me. Come on, Duke, give me your shoulders."

"Jesus," Duke muttered. He moved in under Tracker and the big man planted his feet on the smaller man's shoulders. "Christ, you're gonna break my—"

"Hold still while I try the window!" Tracker hissed.

"I'm trying," Duke whispered back. His shoulders felt as if they were going to break.

Tracker took hold of the window and tried sliding it up. He was pleasantly surprised when it moved freely.

"It's open!" he said. He pushed it up as high as he could, then let it go gradually, just in case it had a tendency to come crashing down again. When it stayed up he got a firm grip on each side of the window frame and hauled himself up and in.

The room he was in seemed to be a storeroom, with boxes and cartons. He could hear voices from the next room and the shuffling feet of the men in the ring.

He stuck his head out the window and said, "Stay there and keep your eyes open. We may have to move fast if someone spots one of us."

"Tell me about it," Duke replied.

After a second thought, Tracker said, "Duke if something goes wrong, you get out of here fast."

"What about you?"

"I'll meet you back at the hotel."

"Okay," Duke agreed reluctantly. "Be careful."

"Yeah."

Tracker lowered the window, leaving it about an inch ajar, so he could get his fingers under it and slide it open in a hurry if he had to. Then he turned and gave his full attention to the room he was in. Once he was satisfied that he was alone, he moved to the doorway and peered into the next room.

It was a high-ceilinged room with a ring set up right in the middle of the floor. There were two men working out on it, and four men outside of it, watching. Tracker recognized only one of the men.

It was Dan Logan.

"How does he look?" Logan was asking a smaller man who was standing next to him. Tracker could hear them very clearly.

"He's as good as he's gonna get," the man answered, and there was something familiar about his voice. "I'd just like to get this thing over with. I hired on to train a fighter. Nobody said anything about any killings."

"There was only supposed to be one killing," Logan answered. "Tracker."

"Yeah, well, he got your men, and he knows my name, so I ain't feeling too comfortable about the whole thing."

"He doesn't know what you look like, Frank, so don't worry," Logan told him.

Frank! That was the third man in the alley. "Frank" was Homer "Kid" Barrow's trainer.

"I don't know why the old man had to mess with Will Sullivan, anyway," Frank went on. "The Kid can beat that old pug easily."

"We've been all through this, Parker," Logan said. "If you ain't gonna tell that to the old man, then keep quiet about it."

"Okay, okay. Hey, Kid, keep that damned left up, all right? You ain't gonna be fighting no sparring partner Saturday!"

Frank Parker folded his arms and directed his full attention to the action in the ring. Tracker settled down by the door to watch, also. He didn't like what he saw.

Kid Barrow seemed to have good hand speed, good foot speed, and there was something else that nobody had told him. Sullivan might have known but Tracker didn't.

The Kid was left-handed.

What the hell was wrong with Will anyway? Why wouldn't he have told Tracker something that was that important so they could work on it?

148

Tracker was satisfied with most of the things he had found out and was getting ready to leave when he heard some commotion outside. First the sounds of a scuffle, and then something came crashing loudly through the window.

"What the hell was that?" Dan Logan's voice asked.

"It came from the other room!" another voice shouted.

Tracker didn't know what had happened outside, but Duke was on his own. He had to get out of this room now, before the men from the other room found him.

He was about to start for the window when he heard the shots from the alley. Those shots could mean two things.

Duke could be dead, and if that was the case, then Tracker was trapped!

Chapter 37

Tracker didn't have much choice in the matter. The pounding of feet from the other room told him that all of the men from that room were on their way to the room where he was hiding. He was going to have to take his chance with the alley.

He ran across the room, slid the window open, and just as a lamp was lit in the room he lifted his legs through the window and jumped down.

He landed on something—someone, actually—and went sprawling across the ground. His first instinct was to turn the body over to see if it was Duke, but a couple of heads poked themselves out the window he'd just come through and someone shouted, "There he is! It's Tracker!"

As a pair of hands came out the window holding guns Tracker got up and started running down the alley. He heard a couple of shots, and chunks of hot metal filled the air around him. The darkness helped, and he turned the corner without being hit.

"Go get him, damnit!" he heard somebody yell, and

he knew that at least a couple of them would be coming out the window after him, while the rest would probably try to cut him off out front.

When he came out of the alley he turned in the opposite direction from the front of the building. As he started running down the street he heard them come out the front door and out from the alley.

"He's going the other way!" someone shouted, and Tracker heard footsteps take off after him.

It went against Tracker's grain to run, but to turn and face as many as five men would have been foolhardy. He'd found out the answer to a couple of his questions, and now he had to stay alive so that he could put them to the best use.

It was late at night, and the streets in this part of town were deserted. Not even the sound of shots being fired changed that.

Tracker did not draw his gun. He simply ran, trying to avoid a shootout. While running, though, he couldn't help but wonder if the man in the alley had been Duke. That little con man was the closest thing to a friend he had, although he'd never have admitted as much to him.

Unfamiliar with the town, Tracker had no idea where he was running to. He just knew he was running away. His pursuers, on the other hand, must have known the streets well, and if he kept running, eventually they might maneuver him so that he ran right into them. He needed to find a spot where he could hide out for a while, and then maybe double back behind them.

He turned a corner and stopped, listening intently. Through the darkness behind him he could hear them still coming, calling to each other and cursing aloud.

When they hit this corner they'd have three choices as to which way to pursue—straight ahead, left or right. Tracker turned left, and almost immediately found an alley, which he ducked into.

It was pitch dark, and he slowed to a walk, so he wouldn't knock anything over and give away his position. Eventually, he came out into a sort of courtyard formed by three different buildings.

He heard someone run past the mouth of the alley, and then heard voices, shouting to each other to split up. It wouldn't be too long before they would double back and try to figure out which way he had gone. He could wait there and hope they missed the alley, but he started trying doors, hoping to gain entry to one of the buildings, walk through it and come out the front door, on a totally different street.

Three locked doors took care of that idea, however. Three sturdy doors, too. Nothing short of shooting the locks would open them, and also give away his position. He could always do that if they started down the alley, because they'd discover where he was soon enough.

He flattened himself against the side of a building and waited, listening. They must have split up—two, two and one, all going in separate directions. If he tried to leave the alley now, he would undoubtedly run into one or two of them. He chose to stay where he was and wait and see.

Shortly, he heard footsteps returning. He drew his gun. If and when they started down the alley, he'd shoot the lock off one of the doors and try to escape through the building.

He waited with his gun cocked, feeling calm because he knew what he was going to do. He wasn't afraid to engage his pursuers, he just didn't see the profit in it at the moment. Of course, very shortly, it could become necessary, but until then...

Now he could hear voices asking who had seen him, who had heard him, where'd he gone. He leveled his gun at the door lock, waiting for someone's silhouette to appear in the alley.

He could still hear them out there, congregating right by the mouth of the alley. He stood with his head pointing one way, his gun pointed the other. Finally, a shadow fell across the entrance to the alley as one of them, with gun drawn, led the way into the alley. A quick shot would have made one less man chasing him, but it wouldn't accomplish all that much. He turned his head, and as he prepared to fire at the lock he heard a click and saw the door swing open inward.

There was no light coming from inside, but he had no trouble recognizing the face of the person who had opened the door.

"Well, what are you waiting for?" Shana Sullivan asked.

Chapter 38

He holstered his gun and stepped swiftly past her, and she closed and locked the door behind them. They stood close together in the darkness, listening intently.

"Where the hell could he have gone?" a voice asked.

"Try these doors."

One of them rattled the door Tracker and Shana were standing behind, as someone else tried the other doors.

"That's it, damnit," a voice snapped. It sounded like Dan Logan. "We lost him."

"Should we go back—"

"Parker, you take the kid back before he catches cold or something," Dan Logan said. "The rest of us will circle around and see if we can find him. He's got to be around, and he doesn't know the area. If we get lucky, he'll run right into us."

After a few moments there were no further sounds from the courtyard, and Shana whispered, "I think they're gone."

"How did you—," he started, but she touched her fingers to his lips.

"Come with me," she said. She took his hand and led him down the hall to a stairway, and then up the stairs. They walked along another corridor until they came to a door that she opened with a key.

"My room," she said in her normal voice. "You can stay here for a while."

Since Logan planned to keep canvassing the area, Tracker decided to accept her offer.

"No light," he said as she closed the door behind them.

"We won't need any light," she said, moving in close to him. He put one arm around her, and with his other hand pulled aside the curtain so he could peer out the window. The dimly lit streets seemed empty, and if they stayed that way for a decent interval of time, he would leave.

"How did you know where I was?" he asked her, still looking out the window.

She was pressing her body against his so that she could also look out the window. At any other time, he probably would have taken her to bed to pass the time, but he was still thinking about the fallen man in the alley.

"I heard the shots," she answered. "I looked out the window and the first person I saw was you. You're not hard to recognize you know, even at night."

"Go on," he said because he wanted to hear her explanation. He was not a man who believed in coincidence. That this appeared to be one bothered him.

"I saw you go down the alley, and then I saw the others. It wasn't very hard to figure out what was going on. Didn't you know you were in my section of the city?"

"I don't know what goddamned section of the city I'm in," he snapped, "but I'm getting the feeling that I was brought here by the lead rein."

He removed his arm from her waist and walked to the center of the room.

"Do you want a drink?" she asked.

"Yeah, thanks."

She got a glass and a bottle, and poured him a healthy drink. He tasted it and coughed.

"Irish whiskey," she told him, smiling.

He turned the glass up and finished it, liking the way it bit as it went down.

"Finish your explanation," he said.

She shrugged and said, "It's finished. I knew you were in the courtyard, I knew all of the back doors were locked. I knew you were trapped, and I knew how to help you."

She knew a lot, he thought. Did she know he was coming to this part of town? No, how could she? There was no reason to suspect her of anything other than being in the right place at the right time—for him.

He handed her the glass and she refilled it and gave it back to him. He took it and moved back to the window.

She moved up against him again and asked, "Want to take your mind off it for a while?"

His first instinct was to put her off until another time, but he made the mistake of looking at her, and her brilliant green eyes and fiery red mane changed his mind.

"I guess I'm relatively safe here," he said.

She laughed—a low, sexy sound—and said, "Not from me you're not."

She slid her arms around his neck and began to pull him down to her so she could mold her pliant lips against his. He could feel the heat of her body right through her clothing, and a fire raged in his loins.

"You need to lie down," she whispered, tugging him along with her to her bed.

"And rest?" he asked.

"Mister, you're not going to get any rest here," she told him. With her arms still around his neck she used all of her weight to pull him down to the bed with her, then climbed atop him and began to undo his clothing while continuing to kiss him. She wasn't just kissing him, though—she was devouring him. She was using her lips and her teeth and her tongue, stopping only long enough to tug his pants and underthings off, then climbing right back on top of him.

"Jesus, you're hot," he told her, as she removed her own clothing and pressed her flesh against his.

"I'm going to warm you," she said. "I'm going to burn you."

She raised herself and engulfed his penis hungrily, causing him to groan out loud.

"Ooh," she said, "you're so hard, so big..."

He wrapped his arms around her, pulling her down to him and then turned both of them so that he was on top.

"Bully," she said into his ear before biting it.

"Wench," he replied. He eased his hands underneath her so that he could cup her buttocks and then began to knead them as he drove into her.

"God," she moaned, "*you're* setting *me* on fire!"

He drove into her at increasing speed until finally he felt her spasm beneath him, and then released himself and began to spurt into her. Each time he thought he was finished she would use her muscles to grab him and milk him for more, until there was no more to give.

"You've ruined me," she said afterward, while they still lay entwined.

"How so?"

"I love the way you feel on top of me," she said, squeezing him tightly to her. "I'll never be able to make love to a man under two hundred pounds again."

He laughed, kissed her lightly, then disentangled himself from her and stood up to dress. While she was dressing he walked to the window and looked down at the street, which was still empty.

Coming up beside him she asked, "Would you like to spend the night?"

Still watching the street he said, "Any other time I'd jump at the offer, honey."

"Was it bad?"

"I had a...a friend with me, and he may be dead. I won't know for sure until I get back to my hotel."

"I'm sorry," she said, encircling his waist with her arms. He looked down at her and held her close with one arm again.

"Yeah, so am I."

"Would you like to rest?" she asked him. "I'll watch the street for you."

"That's okay," he said. "I'm fine."

"Food?"

He shook his head.

"Nothing. With a little luck, I'll leave in fifteen minutes, maybe a half an hour."

She was quiet a moment, then said, "I have an idea."

He looked at her and asked, "What?"

"If you'll give me some money, I could get a cab to come around front. You wouldn't have to walk anywhere, just hop right in and go back to your hotel."

It was a good idea. He gave her the money without question, but she felt a need to explain.

"They don't usually come down these blocks on their own, but if I show him the money, one of them will come."

"Fine," he said. He gathered her into his arms and kissed her soundly. "Thanks, Shana."

"You still owe me," she said, touching his chin. "I'll collect later."

"I'll pay," he promised.

She left, and if he still suspected her, he might have expected her to come back with Logan, but he decided to trust her.

He watched the street and saw her come out and start off to the right. Ten minutes went by, and there was still no sign of Logan or his men. A few more moments, and he could hear the clip-clop of a horse's hooves on the cobble-stoned streets. They became louder and louder until he saw the carriage turn the corner, and then stop in front of his building.

There was a long moment, maybe a few seconds, when he wondered who would step out of that cab, but then the door opened and he saw Shana's flaming red hair as she hurried into the building. She used her key to enter the room, and he hugged her tightly.

"I'll see you Saturday," he told her.

"Is he going to fight?" she asked.

"He's thinking it over, Shana, seriously, but I think the final decision has to be his. It's his life."

"Tracker—," she started.

"Give him these next couple of days, Shana," he advised her.

"Where is he staying?" she asked. "He has a room here, but he hasn't been home in a week."

"He's sleeping in that back room where he's been training," Tracker said. "Give him till Friday night,

157

Shana, then come by. We'll see what we can do. All right?"

She put her forehead against his chest for a moment, then looked up at his face and said, "All right, Tracker."

He squeezed her tightly again, and then left.

He stopped at the front entrance of the building and looked both ways before exiting, while the driver of the cab watched him curiously. He hopped into the cab and gave the driver the address of Farrell House, telling him it was off Portsmouth Square.

"I know where it is," the driver said.

Tracker sat back and held his gun in his lap. He hoped that when he got back to Farrell House he would find a Farrell waiting for him.

Maybe that wasn't such a bad name for a hotel, after all.

Chapter 39

The cab dropped Tracker off right in front of the hotel, and he holstered his gun and stepped out.

"Tracker!" he heard someone shout. He looked up and saw Deirdre Long standing in the doorway of the hotel, waving to him. As he raised his hand to wave back there was a shot and a bullet imbedded itself in the side of the coach, just inches from his head. Tracker hit the ground rolling, and came up with his gun in his hand. The driver of the coach jumped down to the street in time to catch a bullet in the chest.

"Tracker!" Deirdre shouted again, and she started down the steps to the street.

"Stay there, Deirdre!" Tracker shouted at her, but she kept coming out of concern for him. He cursed, got up and started running for her. Bullets chewed up the ground behind him, always a step behind as he scooped Deirdre up in his arms and carried her back to the entrance of the hotel.

"Now stay here, damnit!" he shouted at her.

"You're all right?" she asked him.

"I'm fine, damnit!" he said. "Just stay here!"

"All right!"

Gun in hand he inched his way back down the steps, looking up towards the rooftop for the sniper. He sneaked a glance at the driver of the coach, only to see he wasn't moving. He'd been unfortunate enough to catch a bullet meant for Tracker, and he'd paid the ultimate price.

Another shot took Tracker's hat off, and he turned his head in time to see the rifleman pull back from the ledge.

He was on the roof of the hotel!

"Tracker!" another voice called. He looked up at the hotel entrance and saw Duke, with his gun in his hand.

"Duke!" he called. He was glad to see his friend alive, but he didn't have time to dwell on that feeling now.

"Where is he?" Duke shouted.

"Roof," Tracker called back, pointing to indicate the hotel roof. Duke nodded, waved and ran back into the building.

Tracker moved back up on the boardwalk and moved further on down before stepping into the street again. He saw the rifleman standing up, and knew he was looking for his target. Tracker extended his right arm, his gun arm, and steadied with the left hand. He squeezed off a shot just as the man spotted him and pulled back.

"Shit!" he hissed to himself. Now that the guy knew he had been spotted he would be looking for a way down. Duke would have covered any escape inside the building, so the man would have to find another way. The only place he would go was to the adjoining building, which was one floor shorter than the hotel. From there he'd have to find a way down and, if he remembered correctly, the best way was in back of the building. There was no alley between the two buildings, so the shortest way to the back would be through the hotel.

"Where are you going?" Deirdre asked as he rushed past her into the hotel lobby.

"Out the back," he said. He kept going, past the desk, through the desk clerk's room, into a back hall and out the back door. When he broke out through the back door he looked quickly to his right, his gun extended in front of him.

"Down the back, Tracker!" he heard Duke yell from the roof.

Sure enough, a man with a rifle dropped down to the ground from the second floor of the other building.

"Hold it!" Tracker shouted. He didn't fire immediately, because if somehow it was the wrong man, he could have ended up in a lot of trouble. However, when the man turned and fired blindly with his rifle, Tracker no longer felt any reluctance. He levered back the hammer of his .45 and fired, very deliberately. The bullet struck the man solidly, turning him completely around and causing him to drop his rifle as he fell to the ground.

"Tracker!" Duke shouted again.

"I'm okay!" Tracker shouted back. He approached the fallen man, still holding his gun out in front of him. When he reached the body he turned it over with his foot.

"Danny—," the man started in a hoarse whisper, and then he died. Tracker bent over him and examined his body. He had plugged the man dead center.

Tracker heard footsteps behind him and turned quickly, gun ready.

"Hey, easy," Duke said, holding his hand out.

Tracker relaxed his gun hand and said, "You're alive."

"Of course I'm alive. Who's this guy?"

"I haven't looked yet," Tracker said. He holstered his gun, grabbed the dead man by the ankles and dragged him away from the building to where there was more light.

"See his face?" Tracker asked.

"Yeah."

He dropped the man's ankles and they both took a look at his face.

"I don't know him," Tracker said.

"Neither do I," Duke replied.

"But he did try to kill me," Tracker said.

"A pretty damned good try, too."

They stared at each other for a few seconds, and then Tracker said, "He's got to be one of Barrow's men."

"Maybe he was just hired for this," Duke suggested.

"Yeah," Tracker said, running his thumbnail over his bottom lip. "Where's his rifle?"

They looked around, and then Duke spotted it and

went over to pick it up. He handed it to Tracker, who recognized it as a Winchester 73.

"This is an expensive rifle for somebody dressed like this guy," he said to Duke.

"That means that somebody gave it to him for this job," Duke surmised, "to kill you."

"Yeah. What's happening out front?"

"Why don't we go and find out?" Duke suggested.

"Right," Tracker said. "Let's."

"What should we do with him?"

Tracker looked down at the dead man and said, "Him? We leave him there. Maybe he'll sprout roots and give something back to the earth that spawned him."

Duke gave Tracker a puzzled look and said, "Say that again?"

"The hell with him."

They returned to the rear door of the hotel and made their way back to the front, where Deirdre was waiting.

"Are you two all right?" she asked.

"We're fine," Tracker assured her. "What's going on out front?"

"The police have arrived. Did you catch whoever it was?"

"He's dead," Duke said.

"Oh. Who was he?"

They both shrugged and Tracker said, "We don't know." He turned to Duke and said, "We'd better get out there."

There was quite a commotion out front when Tracker and Duke exited the hotel. As Deirdre had mentioned, the police had arrived. In fact, there were quite a few policemen from San Francisco's young police department.

"Oh, baby," Duke said.

"What?"

"You got your wallet with you?"

Tracker stared at him and said, "Why?"

"Look at all those badges," Duke explained.

"So?"

"Man, these guys aren't going to come cheap," he told his friend. "This is going to cost us a small fortune."

162

Chapter 40

Duke was right, it did cost them a lot of money, but they managed to avoid being taken in to the police station. They "convinced" the police that the death of the driver was an unfortunate accident, and the killing of the rifleman was justifiable.

"Our superior may want to ask a few questions," one of the lawmen said.

"Fine," Tracker replied, "we'll be happy to answer them, if and when the time comes."

That satisfied the officer, and he went off to split with his fellow officers.

A half hour after the incident, the coach was gone from the front of the hotel and so were the crowds. Tracker, Duke and Deirdre all went to Tracker's suite.

"What happened in that alley?" Tracker asked.

"From what I can figure, they were waiting for us," Duke explained. "I guess they waited for you to go inside, because as soon as you did, one man came into the alley and got the drop on me. I got him with this," he added. He shot his right cuff, and a small .41-caliber Derringer appeared in his hand.

"I heard more than one shot."

"When my shot hit him, he fired, but wildly. I picked up his gun and threw it through the window to warn you, and then I took off."

"You left him there—," Deirdre started to accuse him, but Tracker cut her off before she could say something harsh.

"That's the way we worked it, Deirdre," he explained. "In case of trouble, every man for himself. Duke did a lot by throwing that gun through the window and they chased me a few blocks until I, uh, found a place to hide." He had almost mentioned Shana Sullivan, but he changed his mind at the last minute. He wasn't sure how Deirdre would have reacted, so he thought it best to avoid all mention of Will's sister.

"They must have figured I'd come back here," he went on, "and they sent one man to wait for me with a rifle."

"When Duke came back without you, I don't mind telling you I became frantic," Deirdre confessed.

"I appreciate your concern," Tracker replied, "but next time I tell you to stay put, you stay put."

"Since when do you *tell* me what to do?" she demanded. "If I want to worry, damnit, I'll worry!"

"And you might have gotten me killed," he continued, "worrying about you getting hurt instead of myself. That's why we work every man—and woman—for themselves."

Her eyes brightened for a moment, at the thought that he might have been more worried for her than for himself, but then she went back on the defense, not wanting to give in to him.

"If that's the way you want it, Tracker, then that's the way I'll do it next time." She poked him in the chest, then said, "Every man—and woman—for themselves," and stalked off.

"What are we going to do about all of this, Tracker?" Duke asked.

"Well, I don't think the police are going to be much help," he replied. "If we've got enough money to buy off the street law, I'm sure Barrow has enough to buy off their bosses. We'll have to take care of it ourselves."

"How?"

"Now there's a good question for you."

"The fight's Saturday. If Will beats Barrow's kid, that'll make all Lucas Barrow's work for nothing."

Tracker finally admitted what he'd been feeling for some time. It had solidified itself in his mind when he saw Homer Barrow that night.

"Will can't beat Barrow, Duke. I saw the Kid tonight, and Will would need a pole ax to take him."

"Oh. I guess Barrow gets his way then, huh?"

"Not as long as I'm walking on two feet," Tracker said. "That makes three times his men have tried to kill me, and twice in one night. I'm getting tired of playing target."

"So, what do we do?"

"We've got to make sure Homer Barrow loses Saturday," Tracker told him.

"How? You just said—"

"I know what I just said, Duke," Tracker interrupted him. "But Homer "Kid" Barrow is going to lose that fight Saturday, even if I have to fight him myself."

Chapter 41

"Do you really think that man was sent by Barrow?" Deirdre asked sometime later. They had just finished making love and were resting side by side in Tracker's bed.

"That rifle cost too much for a tramp like him to be carrying," Tracker answered, "and on top of that, he couldn't even shoot straight with it. No, it was given to him all right, and it had to be by Barrow, or Barrow's bodyguard."

"His bodyguard?"

"Dan Logan. Barrow wouldn't dirty his hands by dealing with people like the three men I've killed so far. He'd have Logan do it for him."

"You've killed men before, haven't you?" she asked suddenly.

"What?" he asked, caught off balance by the question. "Why do you ask that?"

"Oh, I don't know," she said, cuddling closer to him. "You don't seem that concerned over having killed three men, and maybe having to kill more."

"I guess you wouldn't have run into much killing, working cons with your father," he remarked.

"No, the only kind of killing we made was when we took a mark for all he had."

"And did it bother you?"

She stopped for a moment, and then said, "At first, yes, but after a while you get used to it."

"It's the same thing with me," he explained.

"But...killing—," Deirdre said, stopping herself short. She was going little girl on him. He liked her better when she was hard-nosed and stubborn.

"That was my job for a long time, Deirdre," he said, not holding back. It was time for her to wake up and find out who she was partners with. This, as much as anything else, would decide whether or not Tracker would keep fifty-one percent of the hotel.

"What?"

"I was a bounty hunter for a long time, Deirdre. Dead or alive, that's what the posters always said, only it seemed like they never wanted to come with me alive. Got so I was expecting to have to kill to do my job." He stopped a moment, then added, "Maybe it even got so I was hoping I would."

"Track—"

"Let me finish," he said. "One day I had a poster on a kid. He was about seventeen, eighteen. He'd been part of a gang that robbed a bank. His poster didn't say dead or alive, but I almost killed him anyway, and that's when I realized that I'd had enough."

He fell silent then, but she waited without speaking, not wanting to break the spell.

"That was a couple of years ago. Since then, I've been in a different line of work."

"What kind?" she asked.

He explained to her the kind of "salvage" work he did, and she started laughing softly.

"What's so funny?" he asked her.

"You mean to say, if I worked a con on someone for all they were worth, they might hire you to get it back for them?"

"I guess that's about right," he admitted, and then he laughed a bit himself. "Ironic, huh?"

"I guess it's a good thing I've gone straight," she said.

"After I'm finished with Barrow, I figure to work from here," he explained, "using the hotel as a home base."

"That sounds fine," she said.

"We'll have to talk, though," he added, "about us."

She touched her hand to his lips and said, "I think I know what you're going to say, Tracker. It's all right. There don't have to be any strings between us. There, does that make it easier?" she asked, removing her hand.

"Yes, a lot easier," he admitted.

"Don't worry. I won't become a clinging female. I'm pretty independent, you know."

"I've noticed."

"Of course," she added, reaching beneath the sheets, "there are certain things that a girl can't do alone."

He had to admit she had a point there.

Chapter 42

The next day Tracker went back to sparring with Will Sullivan, even though there was the chance of opening up the cut on his side. He figured he could always stop the bleeding after the session. Uppermost in his mind was not getting Will ready, but getting himself ready. He'd meant what he said about taking on Homer Barrow himself.

"Switch to a left-handed stance," he told Will during the sparring session.

"What for?"

The real reason was because he knew that Barrow was left-handed, but he told Will, "If you get in trouble, you might be able to confuse the Kid that way."

Will switched to left-handed and they resumed sparring. At the end of the session, Tracker caught Will on the forehead with a whistling overhand right, and Will was on queer street again, as he had been on that first day.

Tracker backed off and waited for Will to shake it

off, and he did, but he had no idea that it had happened again.

"Clean up, Will," Tracker said to him when he got his senses back.

"Huh? Sure, okay. Good workout, Tracker."

"Yeah, good workout," he repeated.

When Will went off to clean up, Duke came up to Tracker and said, "Working yourself into shape?"

"He can't take Barrow's kid, Duke. I'm sure of it. One good shot to the head and it'll all be over for him. I can't let him fight."

"I thought you were the one who said the decision was his," Duke reminded him.

"Not when I know he'll get killed, it isn't."

"So what are you going to tell him?"

"I don't know, but I'll wait until the first day of the fight. I need him to get me in shape."

"In two days?"

"Well, I was in pretty good shape to begin with, wasn't I?" Tracker asked.

"Oh, sure. How big did you say that Kid was?"

"At least as tall as me, but heavier."

"Good luck."

"I'm going to clean up. I'll see you later."

Will was gone and Tracker filled a bucket with water and started cleaning up. There was a knock on the door, and he dried his hands and pulled his gun before telling whoever it was to come in.

When the door opened, Lewis, the clerk, came in. When he saw Tracker's gun pointed at him he nearly fainted.

"Uh, Mr. Tracker..."

Tracker lowered his gun and said, "What is it, Lewis?"

"A message, from Mr. Farrell."

"Well, go ahead."

"He said that you should go to the second floor, and that you would know what for."

The buyer was back!

"Yes, I do. Thank you."

"Uh, you're welcome," Lewis said and hastily backed out of the room.

Tracker hurriedly finished dressing and rushed up to the second floor. He entered the room and crossed to the door that separated it from the "meeting room" they had set up. He opened the door a crack and discovered that he had arrived before any business had started.

"Have you and the lovely Miss Long thought over my offer, Mr. Farrell?" the man named Richard Clark asked.

"We have, and we haven't seen any reason to change our minds," Duke said.

"That's unfortunate," Clark remarked. "Yes, very unfortunate. I would have thought that with all those accidents you've been having, you'd be glad to get this place off your hands."

"You're the one—," Deirdre started, but Duke must have done something to cut her off.

"Are you telling us that if we don't sell, we'll be having more accidents?" Duke asked.

"Now how could I tell you something like that? Can I see the future?" the man asked. "However, it would seem to follow, wouldn't it?"

"Who are you representing?" Duke asked.

"I'm afraid I can't say."

"And I'm afraid I wouldn't even think of selling unless I know who I'm selling to."

"I thought you were definitely against selling."

"The right price makes all the difference," Duke said, "and so does selling to the right man."

Tracker could sense the change that Duke's words brought about in the atmosphere of the room.

"Wait a minute," Clark asked. "What are you trying to pull?"

"I want to know who you represent," Duke replied.

"You don't have to know that. I've been authorized to deal. My principal has other things on his mind."

Tracker chose that moment to pull the door open and walk into the room.

"Like a boxing match?" he asked.

"What?" Clark asked, taking a few steps back at the sight of the big man bearing down on him. "Who is this?"

"My name is Tracker, Mr. Clark," Tracker introduced himself, and he could see that Clark recognized the name. "You can go back to your principal—to Mr.

Barrow—and tell him that I own this hotel, and I intend to hang onto it."

"Tracker—"

"That's right. Tell him I intend to build this place up into a gambling house and take his customers away from him. Tell him all of that, Mr. Clark," Tracker said, pounding the man's chest with his forefinger for emphasis.

Richard Clark turned out to be a rather ordinary-looking man, tall and dark as Duke had said, but harmless looking—and right now, frightened looking as well.

"We have nothing else to talk about, Mr. Clark," Tracker said. He put both hands against the man's chest and pushed him towards the door. "Deliver my message to your boss."

Clark hit the door hard with his back, groped behind him for the door knob, found it and fled from the room.

"Why did you do that?" Duke asked. "Now Barrow will see you as getting in his way again."

"That's what I want," Tracker said. "I want him to see me in his way, no matter which way he turns."

"He'll try to kill you again," Deirdre said.

"And harder than before, I'd bet," Duke added.

Tracker looked at both of them and said, "That's what I'm counting on. And the next time Mr. Barrow lays eyes on me," he continued, "will be when I step into the ring with his son Saturday, and get in his way one last time."

Chapter 43

For the remainder of that day, and all the next, Tracker would not leave the hotel. He didn't want to give Barrow's men a chance for another shot at him until he stepped into that ring. If Lucas Barrow wanted to shoot him down in front of all those spectators, then let him try, but he doubted that would be the case. If anything, Barrow would instruct his son to kill Tracker in the ring, if he could. If not, there was always Dan Logan's gun, which Tracker had heard was supposed to be pretty quick and deadly. All of that remained to be seen.

He had dinner with both Duke and Deirdre, giving them each instructions for the next few days. He wanted the hotel sealed off until the day of the fight. He especially didn't want anyone slipping in the back door. Prospective guests were to be closely examined, and kept an eye on if they were deemed suspicious. If the hotel did not have enough men already on the payroll for all of this, then they were to hire more—being careful, of course, who they hired.

Tracker also wanted Duke to go to the Bella Union

and talk to Luke Short, to see what decisions, if any, he had made.

After dinner Tracker told Deirdre right out that he did not want her to spend the night with him. If an attempt was made on him, he did not want her around. She appeared to accept his reason without question. It was a valid reason, but another was to make sure their relationship would indeed be without strings. He didn't want her at the point where she would expect to spend every night with him.

The next morning he sparred with Will Sullivan once again, for the last time. This was the day he would have to convince the old fighter that his days in the ring were past, and that to step inside the ropes again might mean his death.

Before they started he said, "Will, I have to tell you something."

"What? Have I been hitting you too hard?"

"No, that's not it. Will, I can't let you fight tomorrow."

"What?" Will asked, looking confused. "What are you talking about? I thought you said it was my decision to make."

"I did, but I saw this kid yesterday, Will. He'll kill you."

"Hah, not likely," Sullivan remarked derisively.

"It's true," Tracker insisted.

"You've been training with me, Tracker, you know I can take him," Will Sullivan insisted.

Tracker took the man by the shoulders and said, "You've got to face the truth, Will. You're too slow, you can't take the body shots, and one good punch to the head and you're out of it. If that happens in the ring with him, he'll chop you up into little pieces. Face it, man!"

"No!" Sullivan said, pushing Tracker away. "I'm getting in that ring tomorrow, Tracker, and nobody is going to stop me! Not my sister, and not you. She put you up to this, didn't she?"

"I told her the same thing I told you, Will," Tracker replied, "that it should be your decision, but I've changed my mind. I'm not going to see you go into that ring to get killed. You'll have to go through me first!"

174

Will balled up both of his fists and held them up in front of him.

"I don't want to hurt you, Tracker, but if I have to fight you, I will. Don't try and stand in my way."

"You can't beat me either, Will. I've been taking it easy during these sparring sessions."

"You're a liar!"

They were standing in the center of the ring and Will threw a vicious right that Tracker barely eluded. Having missed, Will was off balance, and as if to bring his point home, Tracker hit him with a hard left to the body. To Will, it felt as if he had been hit by a sledgehammer. He fell to one knee, hugging himself tightly.

"You see?" Tracker said.

"L-lucky punch," Will stammered, fighting to catch his breath.

"Will—," Tracker started, but he stopped when the fighter began to get shakily to his feet. "Come on, Will, stay down. Forget it."

Shaking his head, Will continued to rise, saying, "Nobody ever knocked me out with one punch."

"What about the last fight you had?" Tracker reminded him. "One light punch and you went down for the count."

On his feet now, Will started to shamble towards Tracker like a stunned bear.

"Will, one good punch to the head could end it for good."

"Go ahead," Will said, still coming, "go ahead, hit me, you'll see. I can take a punch."

"Will—," Tracker said warningly, but Sullivan was beyond reason. He'd have to be shown. Tracker only hoped that he wouldn't have to kill him to convince him.

Will threw out a tentative jab, then threw a right cross that Tracker easily parried with an elbow. He drove a half-hearted right into the man's exposed belly, then crossed with a left, catching him on the right cheek—just hard enough, he hoped.

Will staggered to a halt and just stood there, somewhere between standing and falling. Tracker stepped in and grabbed a hold of him, holding him up, but still

175

the fighter didn't move. His eyes were out of focus, and Tracker just held him until he came out of it.

"What happened?" he demanded, looking around.

"I barely touched you, Will, and you went out like a light, on your feet. If that happens in the ring..."

Will stared at Tracker's face, then patted his arm and said, "Okay, I'm okay. You can let go."

Tracker let him go and stepped back. Will straightened up, then walked to the ropes and leaned on the top one.

"What do I do then, Tracker? What about tomorrow?"

Tracker walked to him and put an arm around his shoulders.

"I'm going to fight Homer Barrow, Will, and with your help, I'll beat him." He thought a moment, and then added, "We'll beat him."

"We've only got one day to work," Will pointed out.

"So, we'll just have to work that much harder during the time we've got."

When the man didn't answer right away, Tracker said, "What do you say, Will? I can't do it without you."

Will stared at Tracker, then looked down at his hands. He balled them up at once, then shook his head and opened his hands.

"All right," he finally said, looking Tracker in the eyes. "Let's get to work."

Chapter 44

The fight was to be held in the center of Portsmouth Square, and the ring was easily assembled that morning under the watchful eyes of Luke Short. The fight would start at three that afternoon, and would continue until one man either surrendered or dropped.

Short had called in some special help for this special day, right after he had investigated the allegations voiced to him by Tracker. If Lucas Barrow meant to start any trouble on this day, he would pay dearly for it, of that Luke Short was certain.

Short also had a special squad of men who would make sure that no spectator would be allowed to approach within eye or earshot unless he had a ticket.

The fight was a sellout, and more people than Portsmouth Square could easily hold would turn out. They'd be accommodated on the rooftops of the surrounding buildings. Short had made a deal with those hotel owners, a deal that sweetened his pot considerably, even though he had to pay a small percentage to the various hotels.

What Short did not know was that there was a very special spectator who would be watching the fight from inside one of the hotels. Dan Logan, determined that Tracker would not live out the day, had decided to set himself up inside a hotel that was also owned by his boss, Lucas Barrow. After the fight was over, as soon as he got a clear shot at Tracker, the man would be dead. At that range with his Winchester, Logan knew he wouldn't miss.

Killing Tracker would probably not get him off the hook with Mr. Barrow, who had wanted the man dead *before* the fight, but it would make Logan feel a whole lot better about having to leave San Francisco. Tracker had not come out of his hotel for two whole days, and Logan had been unable to get anywhere near the man. Lucas Barrow would not accept any excuses, so after he killed Tracker, Logan planned to hightail it out of San Francisco, before the rest of Barrow's boys could find him.

Damn that Tracker! He'd ruined a good thing for Logan, and he was going to pay. The first clear shot Logan could get at Tracker from his third-floor window, the man would pay!

After the fight, of course.

Maybe the Barrow kid would win anyway, and Logan wouldn't have to leave.

Yeah, Logan wouldn't pull the trigger until the fight was over, and maybe he wouldn't have to leave town after all.

It would be an interesting fight, because Logan had a lot more than just money riding on it.

A hell of a lot more!

Chapter 45

"Are you sure you want to do this?" Duke asked Tracker.

"Ask me again, Duke," Tracker said. "Go ahead, I dare you."

"Okay, okay, I just don't see the profit in this," Duke told his friend.

"The profit will be in knocking Barrow's son right into his old man's lap," Tracker said.

"If you can do it," Duke said, only half aloud.

Tracker gave Duke a dirty look, and then Will Sullivan entered the room.

Sullivan was dressed to fight, because nobody would know about the switch until the last moment. Tracker would inform Short just before he stepped into the ring to face Homer "Kid" Barrow himself, with Will Sullivan working his corner. Duke was the only one who knew in advance, and he wasn't so sure it was a good idea, but when Tracker made up his mind about something, Duke knew better than to question him on it.

"Are you ready?" Will asked Tracker.

Tracker was dressed normally because he did not

want to give away his plans. Before he stepped into the ring, he would simply peel off his shirts, and enter the ring in his Levi's.

"I'm ready," he replied. "Let's go."

As they walked through the hotel to the front door Deirdre was standing there looking out.

"You can see the crowd in the square from here," she remarked.

Tracker thought he heard a low, rumbling sound and said, "You can just about hear them, too."

"Are we ready?" Deirdre asked.

Tracker looked at her in surprise and said, "You're coming to watch?"

"Well, of course," she answered. "Will works for this hotel, doesn't he? Don't I have to support him?"

"That's right nice of you, ma'am," Will said.

"Not at all, Will. You go in there and knock his head off," she said.

Tracker and Duke both stared at her for a moment, then Tracker touched her elbow and said, "Well, come on, let's get it over with."

"My," she said, "the way you sound, someone would think you were about to fight instead of Will."

Tracker set his jaw and they all continued walking.

As they approached the Square somebody saw them and an aisle miraculously opened up for them leading to the center of the Square and the ring. In the ring Homer Barrow was already waiting, dancing about, poking at the air with his massive fists. Luke Short stood in the center of the ring, hands on hips, watching Tracker and his entourage approach.

Tracker didn't see Short's guns strapped on, but he knew the little gambler had that speical gun in that hideaway pocket, and would be able to produce it in a split second.

A mixture of cheers and jeers went up as Tracker and Will approached their corner. Tracker looked to see who was cheering so loud.

It was Shana Sullivan, who was standing in their corner, waiting for them. Tracker hoped that Shana and Deirdre would not get too deeply in conversation during the fight, or he'd have more than Homer Barrow on his hands.

180

When they reached their corner, Shana threw her arms around her big brother, who told her in a low voice that he wasn't fighting. She then walked to Tracker and said, "Good luck, Tracker."

Deirdre, who heard those words, frowned at Tracker and said, "What does she mean, good luck?"

Duke touched her shoulder and said, "You'll see."

Short came over to the corner and said, "Is your man ready, Tracker?"

Tracker looked up at the gambler and said, "No."

Short frowned and said, "Did I hear you right? Did you say no?"

"That's right," Tracker said. He moved up onto the ring apron so that no one but Short would hear what he had to say.

"My man sustained an injury, Luke, and I'm fighting in his place."

"You?" Short asked, staring at Tracker to see if he was joking. "What kind of an injury—"

"Just announce the substitution, Luke," Tracker suggested. "We don't want a riot on our hands, and that's what we'll have if we try to call this off."

"I can't argue with you there, but do you know what you're doing?" Short asked.

"We'll soon know if I don't," Tracker replied.

He jumped down from the apron, and Short approached the center of the ring. Tracker spotted Lucas Barrow sitting near his son's corner and kept his eyes on the older man during Short's announcement.

"Folks, attention please!" Short shouted, and the crowd immediately fell silent. "We have a slight change of plans, here," he said, and the crowd, sensing something was wrong, started up again, louder than before.

Short stood there with his hands on his hips, glaring at the crowd, and it seemed as if the voices died down one by one until the entire crowd was silent again.

"We have a substitution," Short went on, and Tracker saw Barrow's eyebrows shoot straight up. "Will Sullivan was injured during his final training session, so his sparring partner and manager, Tracker, will step in and take his place. I'll make the introductions now."

Short made the introductions of the participants, presenting "Kid" Barrow, weighing in at 250, and—

after pausing to ask him about it—Tracker, who he introduced as weighing in at 235.

That done, Short, as referee, called out, "Come to the mark please, gentlemen."

Tracker and Barrow walked to the center of the ring, where Short advised them of the rules.

"This bout will be conducted according to Queensbury Rules. There will be no biting, kicking, gouging or foul play of any kind tolerated. I want this to be a clean contest, and may the best man win."

The crowd began to roar with anticipation as both men returned to their corner to prepare for round one.

Luke Short yelled, "Time!" and the first round started.

Tracker moved out to the center of the ring and ran into Homer Barrow's left fist. His head rocked back on his neck, and he felt the blow in his teeth, but his eyes remained clear. He backed away a few steps, aware that the crowd was jeering at him for it, but then they booed anything but a forward move. Crowds usually liked to see two big men stand in the center of the ring and hammer each other until one went down. Tracker wasn't going to play the game that way, no matter how many jeers and boos he heard.

After feinting a few lefts that only touched air, he started to move in again and met another of Barrow's lefts. It jarred him again and again he backed away.

The kid had long arms, longer than Tracker had realized the first time he'd seen him, and Barrow knew how to use them to keep away his opponent. Tracker ran into his jab a few more times, and then during the final second of the round he circled the big kid, trying to figure a way past those long arms.

At the end of the round, both men returned to their corners.

"How do you feel?" Will asked him, massaging his shoulders.

"My face hurts," Tracker told him. "He's got hard hands."

"Yeah, and he knows how to use them," Will added. "Listen, Tracker, you've got to get inside that long left of his, or he'll keep pounding on you with it all day until he can cross with the right and knock you cold."

"Do you have any suggestions?"

"Stay away until I study him," Will said. "Give me some time."

"Time!" Luke Short called out, and the second round began.

Tracker followed Will's instructions, staying away from Barrow, circling him. Sullivan watched the kid closely, looking for any sign of a weakness, something he could give Tracker to work on. As he watched, the kid moved Tracker into a corner and began pounding on his ribs with lefts and rights. Sullivan noticed with satisfaction that Tracker was able to pick off some of the blows with his elbows, but too many of them found their mark, and when Luke Short called for the end of the round, there were red welts on Tracker's ribs as he returned to his corner.

"You were supposed to stay away from him," Will reminded him.

"I know, I know, but he's fast. He kept cutting me off, and then he got me into that corner."

"Well, at least your face got a rest," Sullivan said.

"Yeah, but my ribs feel like cornmeal."

Just before Short called for the beginning of round three, Tracker asked, "Didn't you notice anything?"

"Well, I did notice one thing."

"What?" Tracker asked anxiously.

"You ain't even hit him once, yet."

Tracker stared at Will Sullivan, but before he could speak, the third round began.

Duke Farrell also noticed that his friend had not yet struck a blow against Homer Barrow. He watched and flinched each time the kid's left found Tracker's face, or when Tracker took a blow to the ribs. Now, in the third round, Tracker was trying to use his own left, flicking it out at Barrow's face. As Barrow feinted away from one of Tracker's jabs, Tracker stepped in and hammered a hard right to the kid's midsection. Duke would have cheered, but for the fact that nothing registered on Barrow's face. It was as if he hadn't felt the blow. Duke had seen Tracker hit many men like that, and they had all folded up—until now.

Tracker came back to his corner shaking his head and breathing hard. Duke moved in to speak to him.

"Tracker, maybe you should give this up, huh?" he asked.

Tracker turned his head left and then right before he saw Duke standing there.

"Oh, hi, Duke. Give what up."

"You're not doing too good, you know?"

"Hey, I'm doing better," Tracker argued. He looked at Will and asked, "Ain't I doing better?"

Will looked at Duke and said, "He did hit the guy this round."

"Yeah," Duke replied, "once."

"See?" Tracker said, looking at Duke again.

Duke shook his head and when Short signaled for the start of round four, he hid his eyes.

Deirdre Long wanted to hide her eyes, but she found that she couldn't move her hands up to her face. She watched as Tracker walked out to the center of the ring again, and then watched as his head was snapped back by another Barrow left.

"Hit him back!" she yelled, surprised at her vehemence.

She watched Tracker throw a right that Barrow ducked underneath, and then she saw the kid hit Tracker in the belly and she could have sworn that both of his feet were lifted off the canvas by the force of the blow. She clutched her own stomach and seemed to go short of breath, feeling as if she herself had been hit.

Her breath came back when Short called out the end of the fourth round, and she rushed to Tracker's corner, where Duke was still standing.

"Duke, he's got to stop," she said.

"I already suggested that," he told her. "You try."

"Tracker!" she shouted.

He turned and looked at her and she gasped at the swollen areas on his face.

"Hi, Deirdre."

"Tracker, you've got to stop this. He's going to kill you!"

"You call that support?" he asked her.

"This is crazy!"

"How do you feel?" she heard Will Sullivan ask him.

"How do you think he feels?"

184

"I feel fine," Tracker said to Will. "I think he's getting tired."

"Yeah," Will said, "he's getting tired of hitting you."

"He's getting tired, ain't he?"

"Time!" Luke Short called, and Tracker got up for the fifth round.

Shana Sullivan was grateful to Tracker for keeping her brother from the beating Tracker was now absorbing, but she wondered if Tracker would live long enough for her to show her gratitude.

Actually, as she watched the fifth round progress, Tracker looked a little better. She saw Barrow miss more often than he had in the first four rounds, and he missed because Tracker made him miss. Tracker still didn't land many blows, but then neither did Barrow.

Luke Short noticed a change in the tide of the fight as the sixth round started. For one thing, Tracker seemed to have gotten his second wind, while the Barrow kid was getting arm weary. You can get a lot more tired by swinging and missing than you can by swinging and connecting. Short thought that Barrow's aim was to take Tracker out early, and when that didn't happen, the kid got a little upset with himself, and a little confused. Tracker also did not allow himself to be caught in a corner anymore, and Barrow now had to chase around the ring after him.

At the start of round seven, Lucas Barrow started to feel nervous. Things hadn't gone as planned. First, Logan had been unable to kill Tracker before the fight, and for that he would pay. Then the opponent had changed from Sullivan to Tracker. Barrow felt as if Tracker was being shoved down his throat and was laughing in his face. He had counted on his son knocking Tracker out early, and when that didn't happen, he didn't like the way the kid kept looking over at him instead of watching Tracker every moment. For the first time, Lucas Barrow was starting to have doubts about the outcome of the fight, but there was one more thing he had no doubts about.

He was going to see Tracker dead, one way or another.

There was another man who wanted Tracker dead, and a lot sooner. Dan Logan watched the start of the eighth round from the window of the hotel room he'd taken to watch the fight. He drained the bottle of whiskey he had in one hand while hefting his rifle with the other. The drunker he got, the more he wanted to pick Tracker right off in the center of that ring down there. He dropped an empty bottle and picked up a full one. He laughed to himself as he saw Tracker hit the kid a shot with his right hand. What the hell was Tracker doing in the ring anyway? What had happened to the old guy? Lucas Barrow must have been having a fit, and Logan was sorry he wasn't down there to see it. On second thought, if he was down there, Barrow would be able to see him, and that wouldn't do at all.

Wait a second, he told himself, as an idea struck him. Why should he kill Tracker and then start running from Barrow? Here he was, sitting above the crowd with a rifle in his hands, with the power to solve all of his problems at one time. He laughed as Tracker hit the kid with a left, and opened his second bottle of whiskey.

Yeah, why not put a bullet into Tracker as he stood in the middle of that ring? Wouldn't that be some sight?

As Tracker moved out to the middle of the ring to meet Homer Barrow for the ninth round, he marveled at the change that had come over him after the fourth round. During the fifth round he had discovered something about himself. He was having a good time. The kid hit hard, but after the initial force of the blow, Tracker didn't seem to feel any residual effects. He seemed able to throw off the blows seconds after they were thrown. And as the fight progressed, he seemed to get stronger and stronger while the kid's blows became weaker and weaker.

Now, as he approached the kid for the ninth round, he could see the hurt, tired look in his eyes, and he knew he had him.

He gave the kid the first punch of the round, a right to the head, and when he shook it off and grinned at him, Homer Barrow felt fear.

Homer backed off thinking, What do I have to do to hurt this man? He couldn't believe the way Tracker seemed to be unaffected—no, the way he seemed to *enjoy* being hit. Homer looked over at his father, wanting guidance, and as his eyes left Tracker he felt a blow to his chest, an incredibly hard blow that took his breath away.

How could a man hit that hard, he thought, and that was the last thought of his life.

Tracker had followed Homer Barrow as he backpedaled towards the ropes, unsure of what to do. As the kid's eyes flicked into the crowd to find his father Tracker made a move that saved his life. He stepped sharply to his right, intending to throw a right hand to the side of the kid's head, and as he sidestepped a bullet whizzed past him and thudded into Homer Barrow's massive chest.

The kid sagged against the ropes and Tracker turned quickly to see where the shot had come from.

Lucas Barrow stood up as he saw the blood covering his son's chest, and he too tried to see where the shot came from. It was Tracker who saw Logan first as the man turned his rifle and fired again. Lucas Barrow spotted him just as he fired, and then he too felt a massive blow to his chest that literally stopped his heart.

Logan laughed with drunken satisfaction and turned the rifle again towards the ring, where Tracker stood.

The spectators had all started running for cover, and a few of the less fortunate ones — and less quick — were being trampled by the rest.

Tracker knew that if he jumped from the ring into the crowd some of them might be hit by a bullet intended for him, but he couldn't very well stay there and be a target. Will Sullivan knew that also, and he jumped up into the ring just as Logan fired again. Will threw himself in front of Tracker and the bullet struck him in the right shoulder. He was thrown into Tracker by the force of the impact and they both fell sprawling.

Before Logan could fire again, Tracker saw two men in dark coats leap up onto the ring apron and begin firing up at Dan Logan, along with Luke Short.

Logan was struck by at least five bullets, dropping his rifle out the window, and then following right after it himself. He was dead before he hit the ground.

187

Epilogue

"Our problems may be over," Deirdre Long said three days later, "but I still say they came to a bizarre ending."

"Bizarre or not," Tracker said, "Lucas Barrow is dead, so we won't be having any more accidents."

"It's too bad about the kid," Will Sullivan said. They were sitting at a table in the Farrell House dining room, and Will had his arm in a sling. Also at the table were Duke, Shana Sullivan and Deirdre Long. The two women exchanged appraising glances, when they weren't looking at Tracker.

"I guess the kid never wanted to do anything but fight," Duke Farrell said from his seat across the table from Tracker and Will Sullivan.

"That's what I mean," Will explained. "All he wanted to do was fight, and he got killed for it."

"Well, he got killed by a bullet meant for me," Tracker pointed out, "and all I can say is, better him than me."

"I agree," Deirdre said.

"So do I," Shana chimed in, and both women exchanged glances again. Tracker was sorry he had ended up seated between them.

"Will, that was a very brave thing you did, running into the ring to shield Tracker," Shana said, "but I hope that's the last time I'll see you in a boxing ring."

"I don't know about that," her brother replied. "I might start training fighters. Look at what a great job I did with Tracker."

"Don't look at me," Tracker said. "That was my first and last fight."

"Why?" Will demanded. "You could be—"

"Will!" Tracker said, cutting him off. Very quietly he added, "I liked it too much," and everyone knew it was true. They had all been there and they saw the change that had come over him in the fifth round. It had fascinated Shana, and it had frightened Deirdre, who told him she'd give him her part of the hotel if he promised never to get into the ring again.

He had turned down her offer but told her that he'd already made up his mind not to fight again.

Shana was seated to Tracker's immediate left, and as she put her hand on his arm she drew a long, hard look from Deirdre, who was on his right.

"I'm very grateful to you, Tracker, for what you've done for Will," she said, squeezing his arm.

"We need Will alive to tend bar," Deirdre said to Shana, "and he brings in a lot of customers. He's very popular."

"Of course he is," Shana replied. She knew that her hand on Tracker's arm was bothering Deirdre, so she left it there. Tracker, seemingly unaware of all of that, took the opportunity to reach for his beer with that arm, breaking the contact. Deirdre seized the opportunity, and immediately put her hand on his other arm.

"I guess now we can get to the business at hand," Tracker said.

"Which is?" Duke asked.

"To develop this hotel."

"But into what, that's what worries me," Deirdre said, locking eyes with Tracker.

"We'll discuss that later," Tracker said to her, which pleased her. She gave Shana a slow smile and squeezed Tracker's arm. Shana didn't like it, but there wasn't

189

much she could do about it that night. She had to take Will back home with her, but she felt her time would come. She wasn't going to give in to Deirdre that easily.

"Will, we should be going," she said, rising.

"Okay, little sister," he sighed, standing also. "She is determined to mother me as well as to be my sister," he said to his friends.

"You stay out as long as you have to, Will," Tracker said. "We'll cover for you at the bar."

"Ah, I'll be back in a few days," he assured Tracker, who he now recognized not only as his friend, but his employer, as well.

"No, you won't," Shana told him, and Will's eyes went up to the ceiling.

"Good night, Tracker," Shana said, touching Tracker's shoulder.

"Good night, Shana," he replied, looking up at her. It wouldn't be an easy thing for him to choose between this fiery redhead and the blond Deirdre, Tracker knew. He also knew that he had no intentions of doing so. There was plenty of time for both...

"Good night, Miss Long," Shana said.

"Good night, Miss Sullivan," Deirdre replied, just as formally.

"Jesus," Will said, giving his sister a little push, "g'night, everybody."

When the Sullivans were gone, Deirdre also stood up and said, "I'll be in my room, Tracker, if you want to discuss those ideas of yours."

"I'll be up in a few minutes," he assured her. She bade Duke good night and left.

"You're playing with fire again, Tracker," Duke said.

"Please," Tracker said, holding up one hand, "no lectures on the dangers of women, okay?"

"Fine, fine," Duke said. "I just don't want to see Deirdre get hurt, that's all."

"I have no intentions of hurting her, Papa Duke," Tracker said.

"Cut it out," Duke replied, and they both smiled.

"How long are you going to stay around, Tracker?" he asked, seriously.

"Until something comes up, I guess," he replied. "Let's start building this place up while I'm here, though," he went on. "If I get called away, you can go on with our plans."

"Which aren't made yet," Duke reminded him.

"We'll make them, Duke," Tracker assured him. "Now that we don't have Lucas Barrow to worry about, we'll make them."

"I guess Logan removed a few thorns from our side without intending to, including himself."

"That's okay," Tracker said.

"Did you ever find out who those two men were? The ones who jumped up and started shooting at him with Luke Short?"

"Oh, yeah," Tracker said. "I thought you knew. Luke said he brought in a couple of friends to help out, just in case Barrow tried anything."

"A couple of friends?" Duke asked. "So, who were they?"

Tracker looked at Duke and said, "Wyatt Earp and Bat Masterson."

Duke's eyes widened and he said, "Jesus, some friends to have, huh?"

"They're not my friends, but they sure saved my bacon, not to mention Will Sullivan's."

"Can't argue that," Duke said. He signaled to the waiter for two more beers, and as the man approached he said, "I guess the biggest thing is that we won't be having all those accidents on our minds. As soon as our beers get here, let's toast to no more accidents."

Tracker was about to agree when the waiter, carrying two full beer mugs, tripped on a chair leg and went sprawling across their table, dousing them both with beer.

With suds dripping from his hair, Tracker looked at Duke and said, "Here's to no more accidents."

Made in the USA
Charleston, SC
20 December 2012